Martin Waddell says that *Tango's Baby* is "the most emotionally complex book I have ever written". Set in an unnamed urban environment, rife with poverty and petty crime, the book portrays the relationship between the social misfit Tango and the aloof, attractive Crystal O'Leary – from which unlikely union a baby results. What ensues is bleak, but not entirely black. "The working principle in all my work as a writer is that I do not publish stories that exclude the idea of hope," the author says. "Where is the hope in a tragedy like Tango's? It is in the people, is the only answer I can give. Like Tango himself, they are hapless, sometimes hopeless, often bewildered, but again and again, against all the odds, they strive to help."

Martin Waddell is widely regarded as one of the finest contemporary writers of books for young people. His many fiction titles include *The Life and Loves of Zoë T. Curley*, *The Kidnapping of Suzie Q* and the Irish trilogy *The Beat of the Drum*, *Frankie's Story* and *Starry Night*, which won the Other Award and was shortlisted for the Guardian Children's Fiction Award. Twice Winner of the Smarties Book Prize, Martin Waddell was Ireland's nominee for the prestigious Hans Christian Andersen Award in 2000. He lives with his wife Rosaleen in Newcastle, County Down.

TANGO'S
BABY

MARTIN WADDELL

WALKER BOOKS
AND SUBSIDIARIES
LONDON • BOSTON • SYDNEY

First published 1995 by Walker Books Ltd
87 Vauxhall Walk, London SE11 5HJ

This edition published 2001

2 4 6 8 10 9 7 5 3 1

This book has been typeset in Sabon

Printed in Great Britain by
Cox & Wyman Ltd, Reading, Berkshire

British Library Cataloguing in Publication Data:
a catalogue record for this book is
available from the British Library

ISBN 0-7445-7818-3

This one's for me

MW

CHAPTER ONE

"It's none of your bloody business!" Crystal said angrily. "Sod you, sod school, sod everybody."

"Sod Tango too?" I said, because I wasn't letting her off with it that easy. "You really knotted the poor guy up, didn't you? But you're OK. You're getting on with your life. You got what you needed off him. Now he's flushed down the pan and you—"

"Me? I'm left holding the baby," she said, sourly.

"His *baby*," I said. "Tango's."

Crystal's face flushed, and she took a firmer grip on Baby D, balancing him against the angle of her hip.

"You go on about trying to understand what's happened," she said, slowly, "but you've just made up what it might have been like between me and Brian. Don't you never go falling in love with someone, Chris, 'cause you'll find it works out a lot

7

more complicated than you think. Dangerous old game, love is, when you can't handle it."

"Yeah," I said. "For Tango, *it was*."

There was a long pause. Her eyes were shiny, and her pale cheeks were moist, suddenly.

"You're crying, Crystal?" I said.

"Yeah," she said. "Are you satisfied now, Chris?"

I can feel for Crystal, I don't doubt her tears, but it is poor bloody Tango I'm concerned about; *his* story. A lot of people have said and written things about Brian Tangello, most of them not true. Tango's side of things ought to be told, but Tango being Tango, it never will be now. No one would listen if he tried to tell it his way, so I'm telling it mine, and this is the result – the might-be-true story of Brian Tangello and Crystal O'Leary. That means I've talked to the people round Buffey's Loop who ought to know and done my best to stitch it all together so that it makes a kind of sense. I've had to take a stab at some of the who-did-what and the conversations, because no one will ever know the whole truth except Tango and Crystal, but here goes.

When we were at school, Tango was an oddity. He was over six foot tall, and thin as a rake, with a lop-sided mouth and gold-rim glasses, pale as a lily, with great big hands and feet that made him move like a shambling fork-lift truck. He was large, but he wasn't tough. He survived a lot of flak from the other inmates, but he couldn't take it when the teachers kept putting him down as a no-hoper as well.

"Our dumb *friend* Tangello," from Jock Simpson, looking down through his glasses. "But we must speak kindly of the afflicted, mustn't we?"

"Observe the great white void at the back of the room, which now and then appears to be filled with Mr Tangello. Tread softly, lest we tread on his dreams!" from Harris.

"You moronic cretin, Tangello!" from Sam-Sam in a fury, and Sam-Sam genuinely *liked* him and cared, which says a lot in favour of old Sam-Sam and his tattered Red Flag.

What got Sam-Sam's collapsed socialist back up was that everything seemed to wash over Tango without disturbing his brain. But that is not the way it was. Somewhere behind the big owl-like glasses Tango's pride was taking a terrible drubbing from the sheer cruelty of the verbals.

I can remember him sitting in his chair with his long legs stuck out in the aisle blinking at his persecutors, trying not to look miserable. He wasn't tough like the Bakuli mob: he took two real hammerings from Stevie Bakuli in Year Four, before he got too big to beat. But sometimes he would ham it up for Stevie's benefit, playing stupid tricks like the dead gerbil in the condom, acting dumber than he was. It didn't work. Stevie was back screwing him for a soft sod the day after, and the rest of us laughed along with

Stevie, because that was a matter of survival.

"What did I do?" Tango would say.

"You don't have to do. You just are, piss-face!" Stevie would taunt him.

Tango would shamble off round the sheds, and go talk to the dinner ladies till break was over. They liked him because he was polite and called them "Mrs", and he lugged the bins for them if the caretaker wasn't there.

Leaving year at William Whitlaw School finally broke Tango. If enough people keep saying you are destined for the scrap heap, then you come to believe it, which is what happened to Tango.

"No use me coming down here any more," he told me. "I'm off! I quit!"

"Don't be so thick, Tango!" I told him, despairingly, because I could see the way his mind was working. He had only three mates, me and Melons and Jackie Coney – though he'd have been better off without Jackie. There was nobody else he could talk to but us.

"No one thinks you're thick, Chris, so you're all right," Tango said. "But they all say I am bloody stupid, so maybe I am. I've got a right to be bloody stupid if I want to be, and no one can stop me."

The result was that Tango didn't show up at school for six weeks. He was supposed to be sick in his bed, but Evett knew she had to do something, and in the end she sent the Attendance Man round, and that did for Tango, who was out fixing cars when the man called. He liked fixing cars. He was good at fixing cars. Left to her own devices, Evett would probably have let him go on fixing cars, but the law of the land and her Board of Governors wouldn't let her. That was that.

"I promise I'll try to arrange an Auto Mechanic Course for you when you've finished school, Tangello," Evett told him. "But you've got to stick it out here and do some work. You can't just bug off!"

A may-be-might-be course if he learned to pass exams didn't cut much ice with Tango. He bugged off again, first opportunity.

The Attendance Man had the Social Worker in, all that stuff – stuff which *had* to happen. Tango must have known that it would, but he didn't seem to connect bugging off with the troubles that come with it.

Knock, knock on the Tangellos' door down Bright Street, left turn off the Loop. Sam-Sam representing the school, the Attendance Man, Louise Brennan from the Welfare, all in the little front room, reading the riot act and wanting to make Tango and his grannie sign papers that they didn't understand.

Tango's grannie went up the wall in her wheelchair, did a quick wheelie round the light bulb, and came down again, weeping old grannie tears for her grandson.

"Don't you cry, Gran!" Tango told her after they'd gone. "Don't you cry. I don't want you crying!"

11

"My big Brian! My big baby!"

"I love you, Gran. Don't you cry."

She was hugging him, and he was hugging her, and by this time they were both crying.

"You'd better smarten up your act, Brian!" Auntie Flo Tangello said tartly, not over pleased with all the emoting on her hearth rug.

"They shouldn't have said those things to my gran!" he told her fiercely. "I don't want nobody upsetting my gran."

"You need a boot up your backside, Brian!" Auntie Flo said.

"He's a good boy, my Brian," the old lady managed from her wheelchair. "You promise me you'll do what your teachers say, Brian?"

"Yeah, Gran. Sure Gran. Good as gold," he beamed at her. She beamed back at him. In the background, hard as nails Auntie Flo Tangello must have been grinding her false teeth down to dust. She wasn't a blood auntie, but Mummy and Daddy Tangello weren't in evidence and somehow she'd got landed with Tango and the old lady. The result was that Auntie Flo grudgingly gave them house room in return for Grannie's pension book, and Tango was the one who looked after the old lady, gently lifting her and laying her and mopping up her tears when she cried.

That was the home scene, Tango wiping the old lady's tears and promising to be a good boy. What we got at school was different: Tango doing the Big Man cover-up job he always pulled when the world had him in a panic.

"I have to turn up at school, or they'll send my old grannie to prison in her wheelchair!" he told Melons and me.

"They won't put your grannie in prison!" I told him.

"They'd just fine her and take all her money, and you'd go in care," Melons said.

"She hasn't got any money," Tango said, which was reasonable enough. "I got it taped, anyway. They can't stick this on me, no way! Watch this space! I got plans of my own!"

Melons and I took this for Tango-talk and tried to head it off. Jackie Coney just encouraged it. Not that Tango needed much encouragement. His mind was made up. Attending William Whitlaw was like serving a life sentence to Tango. And for doing what? Nothing, as he saw it.

The outcome was that Tango rolled into school late, got himself logged on the computer, did the two classes up to break and then busted out. He spent the rest of the day, till signing out from school time, round the back of Hank's Autos down the Livingstone Road, just off the Loop. From Tango's point of view it was practical experience, doing what he wanted to do. It made a lot more sense than being yelled at by Sam-Sam. He did driving in the yard when Hank got some old motor to go. Sometimes Hank gave him a few notes for helping and sometimes, when Hank felt mean, he just didn't.

"You should come with me. You'd get driving too, and fixing stuff!" Tango boasted to us.

"You're just cheap labour for Hank!" I told him.

"I'm really useful to Hank, Chris. That's why he tells me to keep coming around and gives me money," Tango boasted.

"Hank and you'll get in trouble if Evett finds out," Melons said.

"So I'm out of prison and you are in!" Tango told us.

"We can't stop him," Melons said to me later. "It's not worth bothering, Chris. He's hopeless, old Tango. He lets Jackie egg him on to muck about, but he won't listen to you or me or anybody else telling him he ought to stick it out round here."

So I didn't bother myself unduly, and that cuts into me now, because of the way it all turned out. I was his mate, and I didn't help him *then*, when maybe I could have. I let the big guy down, and I wasn't around when other people tried to pick up the pieces later and stick them together... Trying to tell his story for him is a weak kind of atonement, when it can't change anything for him.

So far as Tango's planning went, he was acting rationally. He had convinced himself that there was a job for him with Hank when he got free from school. Tango was bright enough to know that there wasn't going to be any *other* job, so he looked on mitching off as a career move, whatever

14

it looked like to old Evett. If he got a job he would be able to look after his grannie properly and he'd buy better clothes and he might build up the courage to chance his luck with Crystal O'Leary.

Tango really, *really* fancied Crystal, even then.

He didn't dare approach her, he just mooned about after her looking hopeless. She'd be in the playcage with Madonna and Myrtle and he'd be standing there, just looking, his tongue hanging out.

"Bug off, Tango. Crystal doesn't fancy you!" from Madonna, when she got fed up with him trotting at their heels.

"Like, who would?" from Myrtle.

They were more forthcoming than Crystal. She ignored him, or tried to. The way Crystal tells it now it was Madonna and Myrtle who treated him as a cluck-head, but that isn't what it looked like to us. It was cruel to watch the big guy trying to get her to take some notice of him, and Crystal and her mates treating him as a giggle.

"Little Miss Frozen Princess," Jackie Coney called Crystal.

Jackie probably tried her, but one thing for sure is that Jackie got nowhere with Crystal O'Leary.

Crystal O'Leary kept herself to her neat little blue-cardigan-and-white-socks self at school. No behind-the-bike-sheds-stuff, no boyfriends or booze, none of Stevie or Jackie's little pills or powders, no discos, no nothing ... certainly nothing that would get Coney going, barring the fact that

15

she was female and blessed with the essential equipment. She tagged along behind Madonna and Myrtle round the Loop, turning up in the San Marino now and then, but she was always the quiet one at the back of the bunch.

Jackie Coney said smouldering fires, all that wink and nod and give-us-a-go verbiage that made up his subtle patter, but Crystal was strictly no dice. Madonna and Myrtle gave Jackie back as good as he gave, but Crystal didn't. She stayed in her shell like some delicate little rock limpet, and let it all wash round her.

Jackie figured little Crystal was saving herself for Mr Right.

What she got, in the end, was Tango.

CHAPTER TWO

Tango and Crystal's story isn't a *school* story, but the things that happened in our last term rolled over into their now-we've-left-school lives with a vengeance.

Most of us were kept busy worrying about exams but the only thing Tango had going was his interest in working with old motors, and getting off with Crystal. Of the two, getting the job looked the more likely, which shows just how wrong you can be.

The final act of Tango-at-school was that somebody supposedly turned informer and tipped Evett off about Hank's Autos. Nobody ever owned up. Personally, I don't think it happened that way. The whole bugging-off dodge was transparent, and Hank's Autos was the place most likely, wasn't it?

"It was Myrtle Abjedi told on you!" Jackie Coney insisted.

Myrtle Abjedi was the one who was caught with the dead gerbil in the condom when Tango was passing it round the room in Sam-Sam's class, so Jackie's story made it sound as if Myrtle was getting her revenge.

Like most of Jackie's stories, there is cause to doubt it.

Myrtle was upset by the gerbil, but not *that* upset. She'd probably never seen a condom with anything in it before. There were plenty of condoms knocking around William Whitlaw. They were used for a lot of things you wouldn't think probable, but not much bonking went on – and if there *was* any bonking, it didn't involve Myrtle. Like Crystal, bonking wasn't part of her creed.

Three of them, Myrtle and Madonna and Crystal, two sixteens and a fourteen-year-old, all virgin snow? Well, yes, that is the way it was. Maybe that is what got them together even though they were in different years, because it went against the usual form round the Loop. Myrtle and Madonna and Crystal were their own little Goody Club in the San Marino, and people knew that and accepted it – everybody but Jackie Coney, that is.

It annoyed Jackie that they didn't fancy him, so he gave them bother when he could, and this Myrtle story was just another Jackie Coney opportunity, nothing more than that.

Once Evett got to know the score she sent Sam-Sam the Teacher Man down to Hank's. Hank saw Sam-Sam coming pattering down

Livingstone Road on his little legs and he told Tango to scarper. Tango hid in the Milkwhite Bread container at the back of Hank's yard, by the canal, and Sam-Sam sniffed about, wanting to know if Hank had any old autos that would go, but all the time spying out for Tango. He was there nearly half an hour.

Then Sam-Sam bought an old windscreen wiper to make up for wasting Hank's time, and went off.

"Coast's clear, son!" Hank told Tango.

"He's a real dim-wit, Sam-Sam!" Tango said, hopping out of his hiding place.

"Yeah, but it's risky," said Hank. "From now on you stay clear of my yard in school hours."

Tango was choked. He could see his one job hope going up the spout. He tried pleading with Hank and then, when that didn't work, he switched over to calling Sam-Sam a lot of names, and then he came rushing out of the yard and up Livingstone Road, almost crying with anger and frustration, and there was Sam-Sam lurking in the San Marino Cafe at the corner of Livingstone and Stanley Street, lying in wait.

Sam-Sam stuffed his pizza in his carrier bag, and he came out and grabbed Tango. So Tango was frog-marched round the Loop to school, hand-cuffed to Sam-Sam and a pizza. That's what it felt like to Tango anyway. Sam-Sam had no handcuffs, but he never let go of Tango.

Tango was immense, and Sam-Sam was tiny, so it really must have been something to see Sam-Sam dragging him down the street, like a koala leading a giraffe to the zoo.

Ms Evett got Tango in her office. Apparently she cut him to ribbons, although he would never admit it.

She knew Tango's weak point was Grannie T, so she may have threatened to have the old grannie shut away in a home or something. There aren't many homes left for neglected grannies, but Evett may have fooled Tango that there were. Evett was a dirty fighter sometimes, especially when she felt that her job was on the line. That is how she got to be Head Warder at a place like William Whitlaw prison camp and poor little Sam-Sam ended up Officer Commanding Ablutions.

We were out in the school playcage waiting for Tango when he came out. The rest had gone home because it was after-school time and in our day nobody stayed. If the Bakuli mob wanted to break windows or burn something they came in off the Loop after dark and did the business then.

"You're alive!" I said.

"Told you you'd get nicked!" Melons put in, glumly.

Tango put on a stupid big-man act that didn't fool anybody.

"All that's happened is I get computered through the day!" he boasted. "Break time, fourth class, and straight after dinner, and sixth, I go to Sam-Sam and get stamped on my card!"

"And…?" said Jackie.

"And nothing!" said Tango. "That makes me a Numero Uno Special Class prisoner, like Stevie Bakuli."

It was all face really. Tango's ears were hot and his eyes were bubbly and wet, as if he was going to burst out crying when he got round the back of the flats.

"It was Myrtle who fingered you," Jackie told Tango, by way of doing him a favour. "She was out to get you over the gerbil in your willy-warmer, and that's a fact. So you and me ought to get Myrtle!"

"Yeah! Yeah! That must be it! 'Cause of my willy-warmer! Get my own back on Myrtle!" Tango said, easily led by Jackie as usual.

"Door-bang her!" Jackie said.

"No way!" I said. "How do you know it was Myrtle, anyway?"

"'Cause of the business with my willy-warmer!" Tango insisted. "Like, Jackie has it right!'

"You don't know that," Melons said uneasily.

Jackie won the argument, of course.

The upshot was that Jackie conned Tango into going door-banging at Myrtle's house, and Melons and I bugged off. That would have been all right, door-banging being kid's stuff, but nobody answered the door, so Jackie didn't get his fun. The next thing was that Jackie took it into his head to do the Abjedi's windowbox. He pulled plants up and broke all the flowerpots. Myrtle's mum only had four flowerpots, so it was a mean and petty thing to do.

"I never knew he was going to do that!" Tango told me.

Tango was upset about it.

"I could get Myrtle's old mum some flower pots or something, maybe," he suggested, miserably. "Make it up to the old lady. I really *like* that old lady. I wouldn't do nothing to hurt her. She gave me grapes for my grannie one time I was in the shop."

"That will make it look as if you did it," I said. "Mrs Abjedi might call in the Race Relations whatsit or the cops. Besides, you haven't got any money to buy flowerpots since you got the shove from Hank's."

"So what do I do?" Tango said.

"You could tell Myrtle the truth," I told Tango. "Tell her it was a joke of Jackie's that went wrong. Tell her it wasn't meant to turn out the way it did, and it wasn't the National Front after her mum because she is black. She knows you're not into that racial stuff, even if Jackie is."

"Naw. Can't do that on Jackie, can I?" Tango said uneasily. He was really sick about it.

Jackie had got cold feet meantime, so he went round Buffey's Loop dropping hints that it was Tango who did the windowbox, not him.

"You did it!" Myrtle said to Tango the next day. She'd come down with her best mate Madonna and found Tango with Jackie Coney in the San Marino.

"Not me," Tango said. "Not me, Myrtle."

"I know it was you," she said. "It was stupid and mean, so it must have been you!"

"That's not very nice, darling," Jackie told her. "You don't mean that."

"I don't feel *nice* about him," Myrtle said, meaning Tango.

Madonna called Tango a string of names, none of them printable.

It was just the two-team, Crystal wasn't there. She had to go see her dad dying in hospital so she missed out. Maybe her not being there, and therefore not ending up a party in the fight with Tango made a difference later, but who knows? Little Crystal was a side-act in the Goody Club anyway. It was Madonna and Myrtle who had stuck together right from first year, when naturally enough Crystal was still at Primary.

"You prove it was Tango then, Donna Rice," Jackie said. "Go on, you prove it!"

"Yeah. Get me in trouble again!" Tango said, morosely.

He was put out, because his only way into the clear was to blame Jackie, and he was too loyal to do that.

Tango said "again" because he had them listed for informing on him being at Hank's, but Madonna and Myrtle didn't pick it up. I doubt if Myrtle ever found out why her mum's flowerpots were done.

Madonna called Tango a bag full of names.

"You know you and Myrtle, Madonna?" Jackie Coney said, butting in to defend Tango, but really not wanting to miss a chance to look like a big man slagging Madonna and Myrtle in front of everybody in the San Marino. "You're a pair of old rat bags!"

Then Jackie made a grab at Madonna and jogged Tango's arm so that Tango's coffee poured down the front of Myrtle's new Marks and Sparks Spring Fashion Event coat.

Myrtle went for Tango. She started pulling his hair while Tango was trying to back off, only he couldn't get free and he didn't know what to do, because he was too big and soft to start thumping girls.

Over went the table, and that brought Bernarde out from the back.

Jackie and Tango were chucked out of the San Marino by Bernarde, Myrtle ended up going weepies in the toilet over the state of her new coat, with Madonna propping her up, and both of them vowing vengeance. Myrtle was red mist angry, all coffee stained and humiliated in front of the entire cast in the San Marino. It left her with one idea set firm in her mind: revenge.

A few months later Crystal's dad went and died on her.

The next bit is the Gospel according to Crystal, before she clammed up on me.

"See, Brian was *there,* Chris," she said. "Nobody else was. I'm on our seat down the canal and

24

I'm weeping buckets because my dad is the only one ever loved me or did anything for me, and Manus and my mum don't give a donkey's that he's dead. So I'm out on the canal bank and Brian was good. Really good. Not talking and that. Just he come and sat down on the seat beside me and he didn't say nothing wrong or try to put his hand up my skirt or anything, and I didn't mind him, not then, because I was all in pieces, and I needed somebody. So I'm sitting there and he's awkward and he doesn't know where to put himself and I think, 'Nobody else ever fancied me and he does and why not?' And that's it. It's a funny way to start but that's how it started. Because he loved me when nobody else did, and my dad was dead."

So she let Tango take her out.

"It was just so I wouldn't be in the house with them at first," she said. "My mum and Manus. And he was good, Brian was. Like suddenly he was different, doing the big man, and silly bits to cheer me up, and he was really really nice. Madonna and Myrtle started taking the piss out of me for going out with him and the funny thing was I'd been hanging round them and slagging Brian too but now I just knew that was wrong so I dumped them, didn't I? And they didn't like it. It was me and Brian, and I didn't care what nobody said about him, because he was older than me and he was going to look after me and he was gentle and he was doing everything there was to please me even if he didn't always get it right … and that's the one thing I'll always say about Brian: he always wanted things right for me. If he had things right for me then nothing else mattered."

So they were sorted.

"Nobody else ever said they loved me before," she said. "But Brian did. He said it just right out, like that: *'I love you, Crystal. I always loved you, like. Even when we was in school and you were being shitty bollocks.'* And I said: *'And I love you too, Brian.'*"

That bit of their story must be right. The romantic way he declared his love fits Tango to a T. So Tango had the girl of his dreams nestling enthusiastically in his arms, even if she was a bit surprised at herself.

Whatever else may be true or untrue, whatever bits of Brian Tangello and Crystal O'Leary's story I've got wrong, Crystal needed Tango, and she loved him ... *then*.

CHAPTER THREE

The death of Crystal's dad and the beginning of her big affair happened after our lot had all finished at William Whitlaw – all but Crystal, that is. She still had time to serve. Madonna had moved on to Henry Taplow to do A levels, Myrtle was stuck with helping in her mum's shop, and Crystal had found her man, so it looked like the Goody Club was finished.

The same group break up thing happened with us. My dad got a job, so we had to move to Somerton. Jackie found himself doing eighteen months inside for dealing. Melons took to sitting at home, with no job and no prospects. The result was that we all got out of touch with Tango.

Jackie got remission, and his arrival back in his own haunts, jaunty as ever, was greeted as fortuitous in one unexpected quarter.

"Just what we needed!" Myrtle told Madonna, when she heard Jackie had been let out early.

"Jackie's big mouth will do the business for us. All we've got to do is point him in the right direction."

It was little girls at school getting their own back on the big lads stuff, that is what it was. The old score with Tango and Jackie still rankled, and on top of that Crystal had dumped them and joined the enemy, so they had worked out a scheme to get even with everybody.

They were going to put a spoke in Tango and Crystal's big romance.

"I regret it more than anything I ever did!" Madonna says now. "How could I pull a cheap stroke like that on Crystal? But it's like you feeling you let Tango down, Chris ... what's done is done, and most of what happened they brought on themselves, so I'm not taking the blame for it, and you should try and see the Tango thing the same way, and not keep on about it."

That is with hindsight. At the time it was all a laugh as far as Madonna and Myrtle were concerned, one of their old tricks left over from pulling pigtails in the playground. If they'd known how far things had got with Crystal and Tango they'd never have done it.

The Sunday morning after Jackie's release, he was wandering over the waste ground, side-stepping the dog droppings. He was sniffing about for some of his old contacts to get business moving again, but nobody was out except Madonna.

Madonna was wheeling her big sister's pram. That made Madonna an auntie. With her dad and her mum and her big sister and the big sister's baby and herself in the three-room flat in Nightingale block there wasn't much room for Madonna, so she sometimes took the pram down in the lift and went for a walk. This time it was on purpose. She'd spotted Jackie from the window, and she was about to plant the poison.

"Guess what happened while you were locked up?" Madonna said, swinging into action on Myrtle's scheme.

"What?" said Jackie.

"Somebody I know fancies Tango!" Madonna said, giving him the eyes.

"You're kidding!" Jackie said.

"Who do you think it is?" said Madonna, jogging the pram. Jackie should have been suspicious. Madonna didn't usually turn it on for people she didn't fancy, but there she was doing it, so he enjoyed it. He wanted to keep the patter going.

"Not *you*?" Jackie blurted out. The thought of Tango hitting the jackpot with Madonna boggled Jackie's mind.

"Me fancy Tango?" Madonna said. "Give over, Jackie! I only go out with men."

"Well who?" said Jackie.

"Why don't you ask Funny Bum?" said Madonna. "Ask Funny Bum Johnston who, she'll tell you." And she swung her hips off, pushing the pram towards Stanley Street, on her way to tell Myrtle they were in business.

"Got you!" she thought.

Jackie Coney sat down on the pile of tyres by Shaftesbury block. Melons came up and started talking and then Jackie broke the big news.

"Tango's got a girl," said Jackie. "We get no jobs and no girls, while Tango sits at home minding his grannie, and it's Tango who gets a girl!"

"Who says?" said Melons. "I never heard."

Melons hadn't been away like Jackie. Melons just hadn't been out much since he left school, because he had no money and his sister had satellite TV. He liked the cartoons and the big girls dropping their ski pants even though they mostly did it talking German. That was Melons' sex life, which he hoped nobody knew about. Jackie hadn't got one, though he let on that he had. Jackie wasn't fooling anyone.

"Madonna says so," Jackie said. "And she ought to know."

Even though she wouldn't let anyone touch her, Madonna had a huge reputation for being the expert on all things sexy. When we were in first year and she got her celebrity nickname, Madonna was fat as a barrel. Things going the way they do, Madonna had turned into a look-alike of the *real* Madonna by the time she was fifteen.

"Tango's in love with Madonna?" gasped Melons.

"No," said Jackie. "Guess who?"

"Who?" said Melons.

"Funny Bum Johnston!" said Jackie. "That's who."

There was a long, long silence while Melons thought about it.

Everybody knew Funny Bum Johnston. She was an antique. Worse than that, she was an antique who'd been passed around, and she looked the part. She was thirty-something but she looked more and she had pink hair and two babies and no man. The only thing she had going was her flat, Number 27 Disraeli block. Sometimes she let people use her flat, and sometimes she used it herself, which is why the Welfare had the two babies off her in care – probably just as well for the babies, too.

"No way!" said Melons. "Funny Bum would eat Tango for dinner, with you and me for afters."

"That's what I thought," said Jackie. "But don't say nothing to Tango, just in case."

"Let's find him!" Melons said. "It'll be a laugh if it turns out to be true!"

They went down to Hank's, but there was no sign of Tango round the Milkwhite Bread container. So they went to the San Marino, even though it was still shut because it was Sunday morning. People tended to hang about outside the San Marino for no reason at all except habit and there being nowhere else, but Tango wasn't there either.

Then they met Funny Bum down by the railings at Cobden Street, just off the end of the Loop. Funny Bum went right past as though she didn't see them, waggling her bottom. Funny Bum is

31

called Funny Bum because she has one leg shorter than the other, which makes her backside jog when she walks.

"Sexy!" Melons cooed.

"Look at that go!" shouted Jackie Coney.

Funny Bum didn't let on that she'd heard them.

"Yo-yo-yo!" Melons yelled.

"Bow-wow-wow!" went old Jackie.

Funny Bum turned round.

"Bug off!" she said.

"Oh, pardon us," said Jackie.

"Pair of little creeps!" Funny Bum said.

"That's not very nice, is it?" said Jackie. "Calling us creeps!"

"That's what you are, Jackie Coney," Funny Bum said.

"How's lover-boy then?" said Jackie, meaning Tango though he didn't say so, because he didn't really believe it … yet.

"Bigger than you!" Funny Bum said, and she gave them both a look which drove them off. There was no way they could mix it with Funny Bum Johnston.

Jackie and Melons went across the waste ground to the dump by the swings. They were mucking about when Tango came along, but he didn't see them.

Tango sat down on the bench by the snapped off cherry tree, just across from the entrance to number three stairs Disraeli, where Funny Bum's flat is.

It was Tango all right, but Tango was different.

He had on new jeans, and he'd had his hair trimmed, and he was twiddling his thumbs and looking even paler than usual. He looked as if he was waiting for somebody.

"It has to be true!" gasped Melons.

"Tango with old Funny Bum!" Jackie muttered, shaking his head. "I get put away for a few months, and look what happens to my mate!"

Tango sat alone on the bench.

Then along came Funny Bum Johnston with Crystal O'Leary. They were an odd couple. Little Crystal was all doe-eyed; dressed up in cream and white like a tiny elf, long gold hair flowing to her waist. Funny Bum was plump, solid, and tottering along on her high high heels, full of bounce.

They stopped and they talked to Tango.

Then Funny Bum Johnston walked away.

That left Tango with Crystal O'Leary.

They sat on the bench, holding hands.

"Do you see what I see?" Jackie Coney asked, in wonderment. "Crystal O'Leary! Tango's bloody dream come true!"

"I do see, but I'm not believing it!" said Melons, enviously.

"Crystal O'Leary!" Jackie said, shaking his head. "All those years he trailed after her, and now... Imagine old Tango and Crystal O'Leary! What's been happening? How did those two get it together?"

"Dunno," said Melons, because he didn't, not

having been out and about since his sister got the satellite.

They sat and they thought.

"Imagine *her* and Tango," said Coney.

"Yeah," said Melons. "Nice though, isn't she?"

"Not very," said Jackie Coney, doing his man of the world strut. "She's just the same skinny little kid she was at school."

"She's still at school," Melons said. "Must be. Because she's not sixteen yet. She's the year behind us. Maybe fifteen now."

"Could be fifteen, just about," Jackie said.

"So what's wrong with us?" Melons burst out, painfully.

"What do you mean us?" said Jackie.

"How come it's Tango she fancies, not us?" Melons said. "I mean, I wouldn't mind some school girl, if I could get one."

"A little kid like Crystal O'Leary?" Jackie Coney said. "You don't fancy shitty old Crystal O'Leary?"

"I don't fancy her minder!" Melons said, injecting a bit of reality. Crystal's brother Manus had an evil reputation for duffing up people.

Tango and Crystal got up off the bench, and they walked over towards the entrance to Disraeli block. Then Tango sat down on the grass and Crystal O'Leary went up the number three stairs.

She had a set of keys in her hand, and her little silvery-white shoes clack-clacked on the concrete steps.

34

Five minutes later Tango got up and went up the stairs after her.

Jackie Coney and Melons didn't know for sure that Tango went to Funny Bum Johnston's flat with Crystal O'Leary, but there was nowhere else in Disraeli block on Tango's list, so it looked like that was where he'd gone.

Jackie Coney and Melons were plain jealous, particularly Jackie, who couldn't figure what had happened during his time away, considering that Crystal had paid no attention to Tango when they were at school. Now she was off into Funny Bum's flat with him, and Jackie Coney was all a-bubble, bursting to spread the news round the Loop, just as Myrtle had planned.

"Crystal and Tango were looking for somewhere private they could go to be together that was better than the Milkwhite Bread container at the back of Hank's yard," Madonna says. "Then up pops Myrtle, seizing the chance she'd been waiting for to screw things up for Tango – well, for both of them, really. She had never really forgiven Crystal for going cool on us and taking up with Tango in the first place."

"I could fix it for you to use Funny Bum's flat," Myrtle told Crystal, as if she was doing Crystal a big favour.

"Yeah!" Crystal said. She was delighted, which shows she wasn't using her skull, considering she knew her Tango wasn't Myrtle's flavour of the week.

Myrtle got them the key to Funny Bum's flat for Sunday mornings, when Funny Bum was off visiting her kids at the foster parents. Using the flat was never a paying arrangement. Myrtle's mum was the one who helped Funny Bum when the Welfare took her kids, so Funny Bum may have felt she owed Myrtle one, but that wasn't the real reason. The real reason was Funny Bum's turning softie when she heard Crystal's story. She wanted life to be all hearts and flowers, and she thought Crystal and Tango looked the part.

At the time, Crystal thought Myrtle had done her a favour, and Tango never smelt a rat, which is typical Tango. Myrtle had calculated that using Funny Bum's flat was one dead sure way of being found out, the people round the flats being as nosy as they are. Jackie Coney being out and about and talking to all and sundry made it double sure. So Myrtle was setting them up. The flat was too close to home. Manus O'Leary would get word of what was going on, and Manus would bang Tango into a jelly. As a result Tango would lose his little wisp of a girlfriend and a lot of face with everybody, both at the same time.

Myrtle shouldn't have done it, and Madonna shouldn't have helped her, but then neither of them knew how far things had gone already.

They had a big shock coming.

CHAPTER FOUR

The Goody Club was re-united at Crystal's request in Myrtle's front room, to cope with an all-girls-together emergency. Crystal wore her school uniform blue top, the other two were in blue as well, though that was just a coincidence which stuck in Madonna's mind.

Crystal, tearful, sitting on the sofa, said, "I'm going to have a baby."

"Whose is it?" Madonna asked.

"Brian's!" came indignantly, from Crystal. "Who do you think I am? I love Brian. I never let anyone else touch me!"

Myrtle's face! Myrtle had stitched up Tango and Crystal to bust their little romance and here was Crystal, with her school bag tucked in beside her, weeping on the sofa, talking about her one true love and a baby on the way. What Myrtle had left out of her calculation was that you don't have to have the key of a flat for use on Sunday mornings to get pregnant, and Crystal was some time gone already when they started going to Funny Bum's.

"Jesus, what'll I do? I've been such a bitch!" an ashen-faced Myrtle asked Madonna, after they had survived the scenery, and got off-side in the kitchen. They were getting little Crystal an instant coffee, Crystal being just a sob on the sofa by this stage.

"There is nothing you *can* do now," Madonna told her simply. "It's too late."

"You took in what she said about her brother Manus?" Myrtle said. "I'd heard he was bad; I never knew he was that bad. If he beats her she might lose her baby. He couldn't do the things she says, could he?"

"I don't know," Madonna said.

Crystal had been having hysterics on the sofa. She was scared of what would happen when brother Manus came back from Glasgow, and heard the news. She'd let out a lot of information that was new to them. Manus had beaten her with his fists once or twice before, and even threatened old Mrs O, his mother.

"I'd never have started it, if I'd known he was that bad," Myrtle said. "Nobody told me the brother was a maniac!"

There was a distinction in Myrtle's mind between a Manus who might be expected to give Tango the usual Buffey's Loop type tap after the pubs closed, and the red, raw mother-and-sister thumping brother who'd emerged in Crystal's account of life at the O'Learys'.

"Well, you should have thought of that before," Madonna said, not very helpfully.

"Crystal wasn't having a baby before," Myrtle said.

Myrtle was working herself into a state.

"Calm down, Myrtle," Madonna told her. "It isn't your fault. You didn't get Crystal pregnant. Tango did that all by his little self. And Manus mightn't care. He might think he'd best leave well alone, if his sister's having a child. Crystal may be exaggerating the danger."

She didn't make it sound convincing, and neither of them were convinced.

"What got to us was that Crystal was absolutely terrified of what her brother would do," Madonna says. "They'd had big, big fights at home before, but they'd kept it quiet, because the mother didn't want Manus going to prison again. We had to believe Crystal was telling the truth. You only had to look at her to know it. She was scared out of her wits of Manus."

"They'll have to run off or something, to get out of his way," Myrtle told Madonna.

"You know that's not going to work," Madonna told her. "We'll just have to tell her to get her mother to put the lid on Manus when he finds out. Surely old Mrs O can manage that?"

Myrtle took the instant coffee in, sat Crystal upright on the sofa and told her straight out: "Everybody knows you and Tango have been using Funny Bum's flat."

"No they don't," Crystal said, through her sniffs. "We were dead careful. You and Madonna and Iris know, nobody else." Funny Bum Johnston's name is Iris.

"Jackie Coney knows," Myrtle told her brutally, determined to get the message across. "Jackie Coney saw you. So did Melons. And if Jackie knows, the world knows. That means your mum is going to know soon and Manus is going to find out when he gets back from Glasgow."

Crystal looked at her as if she was crazy.

"My mum knows already," Crystal said. "She came straight out and asked me. It was me missing periods, and that. I said, 'Oh no, I'm not' because I thought I might not be and she said, 'Oh yes, you are' and we did the kit you get in the chemist's and my paper came out blue, so I am. I *am*, really and truly."

"What does Tango say?" Madonna asked.

"Didn't tell him yet, did I?" Crystal said.

"Well, he'd better be told quick," Myrtle said.

"Don't want to worry him," Crystal said, looking unhappy. "He gets easy upset, my Brian, because he has so much trouble looking after his grannie, and he doesn't need any more of that stuff."

Madonna gave Myrtle a look. Myrtle shrugged hopelessly. They had to really go at her to make her see sense.

"If what you're saying is true, your brother Manus will crucify him!" Madonna said. "It looks like you could get hurt and Tango could be maimed, so someone had better tell him!"

"Don't want to bother him," she mumbled. "Nothing will happen if Manus doesn't find out."

Crystal sat there on Myrtle's mum's pink sofa, blinking at them, twisting her school tie through her frail little fingers.

They took that in.

"But Manus *will* find out, Crystal," Myrtle told her, trying to keep everything calm and reasonable.

She was in a spot, Myrtle.

"One day you're going to walk into the house with a baby in your arms, and then Manus is going to know," Myrtle said.

"Well, I suppose so," said Crystal. "Only my mum said don't tell him yet till we figure something out, so I'm not."

Madonna and Myrtle were getting nowhere.

"So what does your mum intend to do about it?" Myrtle asked, growing impatient.

"Don't know," Crystal said.

"What are *you* going to do about it?" from Madonna, direct as usual. "That's more to the point."

Mumble, mumble from Crystal.

"If you're not too far gone…" Madonna began, hesitantly.

"No!" from Crystal. "No way. I'm not doing that. My Brian wouldn't let me."

"But…"

"It's our baby. My baby and Brian's. And we're

having it." Then she started crying and mumbling again, all the time saying the same thing.

"My mum'll think what to do about Manus when the time comes," Crystal told them.

Crystal didn't seem to take in that there wasn't any time. Manus might not know that there was a baby on the way till it was brought home from the shops in its wrapping paper, but he was going to find out about the business at Funny Bum Johnston's flat the very next time he turned up at number 8 Stanley Street, because there were a lot of kind friends waiting to tell him.

"Mum won't let Manus hurt Tango," Crystal said, after they'd explained it to her for the third time.

"You can't go on relying on your mum for everything, Crystal," Madonna said, with the thought that if Manus had got as far as fisting Crystal and threatening their mother before he had cause, nothing was going to hold him this time.

That didn't seem to sink in either.

"You know what?" Madonna said, when Crystal had gone. "You know what? Crystal hasn't a clue."

'She's just a kid," Myrtle said.

"What if Tango doesn't back her up?" Madonna said. "Do you think he will? He might say the baby isn't his and she can go jump. He'll clear off and Manus will half kill her."

Myrtle made a face.

"It's bad enough either way," Madonna said.

"Little Crystal isn't able to cope, and Mrs O seems to be sitting there on her sixteen-stone butt and doing nothing about it. So I know what I'm going to do."

It shows the guts Madonna had. She put on her coat and she went off to see Mrs O by herself.

Madonna gee-ed up Mrs O to action.

That the big showdown in the San Marino happened so soon was down to Madonna trying to put things right. She thought if everything was sewn up tight when Manus turned up from Glasgow, there might be some hope of Mrs O managing to restrain him.

"If he lays a hand on Crystal I'm going to the cops," Madonna told Mrs O on one of her house visits, because there didn't seem to be any other way.

"Oh, no, dear," from Mrs O, plainly panicky. There followed a lot of verbiage about what a good son Manus had been to her since his poor daddy died, how he'd never have hurt anyone if it hadn't been for the drink, and how he had promised her there would be no more violence after the last time.

Madonna found the recitation chilling, as well she might. Mrs O was telegraphing the information that she'd no hope of stopping Manus, if he took it into his head to start. She didn't mean it to sound that way, but that's the message Madonna felt she was receiving.

"Well, we'll see," Madonna said, uneasily. "But first we have to get everything else on the line."

43

"Yes. I suppose so," Mrs O sniffed, and there were tears brimming in her eyes.

If you ask me, the amazing thing about this scene is Madonna. Just turned seventeen, trying to do her A's at Henry Taplow, and here she was coping with life and death stuff, threatening this old woman that she would put her son behind bars if he laid a finger on Crystal.

That is big stuff.

CHAPTER
FIVE

Tango didn't react to Crystal's revelation in the way most people in his position might have been expected to. I only have Crystal's account of it, as told to Madonna, but apparently big Tango was all over her.

"Like when he used to bug off at school," Madonna says. "He never thought he'd be caught doing it. Same with the baby. He fell for the idea of being a *daddy*, but that was as far as his mind could take it."

Crystal was looking at him with her little peaky face all confused. "But what are we going to do, Brian?"

"Baby! Great! My baby!" Tango is going. "Me! A daddy! Me!"

Delight like that.

"We'll find some place. A flat. Or a house. Some house with a garden. Yeah! For my baby! Great! You and me and the baby…"

"That costs money, Brian!" from a frightened Crystal.

"I'll fix it! Like ... get a job, won't I? Hank will fix me up some big money job. Hank has friends. Some of Hank's friends will give me a job. Hank will fix it, once he knows I'm a daddy!"

"Are you sure, Brian?"

"Yeah. Yeah. Hank knows me and motors. Hank will fix it."

Crystal knew Tango had been working on and off for Hank, nothing regular, but he had money sometimes, and she thought maybe Tango was on the level, this time.

"Settle us down, won't I?" Tango told her. "You and me in our own place with a kid! Me in a regular job! Yeah! Great!"

Then he took her out and bought her a take-away at the Pekin Duck, only it turned out later that he didn't have to pay for it, because he'd done some work on Mr Loe's motor for Hank.

They ended up celebrating back in the Milkwhite Bread container, just the two of them, cuddled up together on Tango's old duvet in the dark.

It was just another Tango-tale of course, but little Crystal bought it. Her big man Tango was going to cope, and she sat back and waited for it all to start happening.

Crystal was floating about on cloud nine, and Madonna couldn't get her to see sense. Over it all there loomed the shadow of Manus, who could be expected home any time.

"I got landed with the nitty gritty," Madonna says. "I was left with sixteen stone of Mrs O quivering with anxiety about her 'he's-a-good-boy-really' son at one end, and Tango buoyed up by the joys of fatherhood at the other. I had to get the two ends to meet before Manus came home. Something had to be done, but I couldn't get them to see it."

"You could have walked away from the problem, Donna," I told her.

"Not when I looked at Crystal's face, I couldn't," Madonna says, with feeling. "She just hadn't a clue. She took Tango at his word. Babies, houses, jobs, Manus, everything. Her Tango was going to smooth it all out, no bother."

It's a feature of Tango's story that people could see his problems coming, and kept trying to help him, but it never seemed to work out the way they intended.

The showdown Madonna planned was arranged for the San Marino and I ended up a spectator, without realizing until halfway through that I was sitting in on something big.

Why the San Marino as a venue?

"Not in your house, no way!" Tango told Crystal.

"Why not?" from Crystal.

"Just, I'm not," from Tango.

It emerged that the meeting couldn't be held at Tangello's, because Tango didn't want his grannie or auntie to know yet. Madonna wasn't going to bring it all home to her mum's flat in Nightingale block, and Mrs O wouldn't be seen dead in a pub, so the San Marino was the only answer.

"Get your mum down here for nine o'clock, Crystal!" Madonna told her.

"She might not come," Crystal said. "It's her prayer meeting night."

Mrs O had got herself wrapped up with this do-gooder religious lot on the estate, where a lady called Sister Monica Rose was helping out with the winos, along with a side-kick who got direct messages from God. I don't know what his real name was but everyone called him the Geek. Those two are important in Tango's story, but just then they seemed like an irrelevance to Madonna.

"She's *got* to come, Crystal!" Madonna said. "Tell her she's got to give the Geek and Sister Monica Rose a miss."

Crystal worked it somehow. She and Mrs O duly turned up in the San Marino, and as it happened, the meeting was scheduled for the only night I'd been there for months. I was on a quick trip back to the Loop after months away up Somerton, and of course I ended up on my own. The place was deserted – nobody there, just me playing the pin-ball machine and a gloomy Bernarde behind the counter.

"Hi, Chris," Madonna said cheerfully. "Long time no see."

"I just nipped back to see people, Donna," I started to tell her, but she had already turned her back. She shepherded an ash-faced Crystal and

Mrs O up to table seven, at the far end, effectively cutting me out. All I registered was that the vibes were bad even to begin with, and they rapidly grew worse.

A quarter of an hour went by, and Mrs O was on her second coffee. She was complaining about something, and in between times she kept looking at her watch.

Then Madonna said something to her.

"Oh, no!" Mrs O said, raising her voice. "We agreed tonight's the night. You get him here."

Madonna flounced down my way, making for the door.

"How's tricks, Donna?" I said.

"Awful," she said. Then she stopped momentarily. "I don't suppose you've seen your bloody mate Tango about, have you?"

"No."

"Well, if you do, tell him I'm going to kill him!" she said, and out she went into the night.

She was off on a Tango-hunt.

I have to admire Madonna slogging her little seventeen-year-old legs round the Loop after dark for more than an hour, with all that would entail, given the fact that she was female and out on her own, and most of the street lights are permanently gone phut as a self-induced convenience for Stevie Bakuli and his mob.

Tango was in the Builders' Arms, on his own, with a can, watching a switched off TV set.

"Where've you been? You're supposed to be

down the San Marino," Madonna told him. "You're not bugging off on this one. Mrs O says it's got to be tonight."

"OK," Tango said, not very steadily. "OK."

Madonna let him have a mouthful of verbals about growing up, for God's sake and all that stuff.

"I've made big plans of my own," Tango told her. "Like, I'll look after Crystal, all right. Not her mum. Me. Because Crystal is my responsibility." There was a touch of pride in his voice when he said it, but Madonna wasn't impressed.

"That's great, Brian. Now what about the meeting you're not at?" Madonna said. She gave him a mouthful about letting her down and letting Crystal down.

"OK. OK," Tango muttered, slurring the words. "I get the message!"

"*Now*, Brian!" Madonna insisted. "Tonight!" It is interesting that she'd begun to call him by his real name. Probably it was because Crystal always called him Brian, and she'd got infected. Nobody ever called him Brian at school except the dinner ladies.

Tango gave in and came with her, but on the way he insisted on grabbing poor Funny Bum out of her flat for moral support. That took longer than Madonna reckoned it would, Funny Bum being Funny Bum, and by the time they landed back in the San Marino, Madonna's time was up. She was in line for execution if she wasn't back in Nightingale by the time the clock struck the hour.

It was part of the deal with her parents, when she wanted to go to Henry Taplow.

"I'm afraid I've got to go, Mrs O'Leary," she said.

Mrs O wasn't paying much heed.

She'd gone stiff when Funny Bum turned up. Presumably she knew Funny Bum's reputation, and it was another score against Tango in her book.

"Some thanks you get, I don't think!" Madonna said to me, on her way out.

This was the big scene then: Mrs O'Leary, Crystal, a hang-dog Tango with several tins in him diluted by Funny Bum's black coffee, and poor Funny Bum, dragged out of her flat to hold the coats.

I'm sitting there, looking like a prune. I'd been hoping Tango or Jackie or Melons would come in so I could catch up on events round the Loop, but it didn't take a lot of perception to realize that Tango was in no mood to chat. He gave me a hang-dog and dismissive "Hi, Chris," when he came in, and I was left marooned, not knowing what was afoot, and trying not to look as if I was listening in. I couldn't hear much because of Bernarde's tapes and his clattering dishes, so most of it took place in elaborate mime, as far as I am concerned.

They were all heads together, and Mrs O was doing the talking.

"No, Mum!" Crystal said.

More mutters.

Then somebody knocked a coffee cup onto the floor.

Bernarde ambled down towards them to cope, and the conversation froze.

Mrs O was looking daggers at Funny Bum.

Bernarde retreated. The whispering began again.

So what was the gist of their heated confab?

As far as I can reconstruct it, it seems absolutely *nothing* was revealed about Tango's "big plan", which is significant in itself. For once in his life Tango knew what he was going to do, and he knew Mrs O wasn't going to like it, so he didn't tell her.

Piecing it together, the talk at table seven appears to have gone something like this:

"You got my daughter pregnant, Brian Tangello, and now what are you going to do about it?" from Mrs Teresa O'Leary.

"Don't tell my grannie," pathetically, from Tango.

"Not to mention your auntie!" very much to the point from Funny Bum, who had brushed against Florence Tangello before.

"Nobody's telling my auntie!" from Tango, in a panic.

Don't tell on me would be his key-note, as if he was still in the playcage at school, and as if the nature of things wasn't such that sooner or later people were going to know.

"Well, we'll just get married, won't we, Brian?" defiantly, from Crystal. "We'll have our wee baby and get married."

"Yes, Crystal. Sure thing. That's the way I want it too, Crystal," from Tango.

"It's not a sure thing at all!" came from Mrs Teresa O'Leary.

And so it went on: lots of recriminations, but all inconclusive. With no Madonna to keep their minds on the matter in hand, there wasn't going to be a meaningful outcome.

Then Mrs O pulled her big clincher out of the bag: Tango was guilty of Unlawful Carnal Knowledge with a Minor.

"You could go to prison for what you've done to my daughter!" was the line.

That isn't necessarily true: there are winks and nods and ways and means, as somebody with Funny Bum's past record should have been able to tell them. Maybe she didn't because all the horror stories about having to name the father in order to get benefit confused her. Funny Bum's experience would pre-date that stuff.

"We'll get married. Then you can't touch us!" from Crystal, ignoring the implications of the threat.

Then came the predictable killer line: "What's going to happen when Manus finds out?" said Mrs O.

Mrs Teresa O'Leary set out her stall: Crystal and Tango had to get rid of the baby, so Manus would never know it had all happened. Then Manus wouldn't get drunk and beat Tango to a pulp, and as a result Manus would stay on the clear side of the cops and not be put away again.

Simple.

"It's my baby, Mum!" tearfully, from Crystal.

"If you don't get rid of it your poor brother will be the one that suffers!" said the sublimely single-minded Mrs O'Leary. Crystal swears she said it.

"No," from Crystal.

"Oh, but yes," from Mrs O'Leary.

Then Crystal pulled her chair back and got up. She came down towards me, and Tango started after her. He grabbed her and hauled her into one of the little side seats by the door. He had his arm round her, and he was talking in her ear. In the middle of it, he looked up and saw me, and he winked, as if to say, "It's a game, isn't it, Chris?"

It didn't look like a game to me, because Crystal was crying and hurt, and clinging onto him... Needless to say, Crystal having *anything* to do with Tango was a new one in my book at the time. I could only take it that all his old playground years of persistence had paid off handsomely.

"What are you doing here, Chris? Snooping?" a tear-stained Crystal said, noticing me for the first time. Tango had got her onto her feet, and she went back to table seven, like she was walking to her death.

"Good seeing you again, Chris," Tango said, patting me on the arm as he passed.

"She all right, Tango?" I nodded in Crystal's direction.

"Yeah. She's fine," he said. "Like ... I'm looking

54

after her, Chris. She's my girl now. No bother, mate."

"If you need any help…" I said.

"Me? No! Cracked it, ain't I?" he said, and he strolled truimphantly off up the aisle, toward the ravaged eyes of his would-be mother-in-law, by now weeping into her cold coffee.

Knowing what I did of Tango's lovelorn pursuit of Crystal in his schooldays, *that* amazed me, and I wanted to know more about it, but the want had to go unsatisfied.

Maybe … maybe if I'd known the full score then, I could have got together with Madonna and shifted it someway, but I don't think so. Buffey's Loop was well out of my life by then, and Tango and Jackie and Melons didn't seem so important any more. Anyway, nothing could have shifted Tango much in that mood. I was left thinking Tango must have got something right if he'd made it with Crystal, and wondering why she'd made her crack about me snooping. Looking back, I think she'd got herself so centred on Tango and how he was going to save her that she didn't want any of his old mates in on the act. *Her* friends Myrtle and Madonna were fine, because they were backing her up and the number she was in was big woman's stuff. Jackie and Melons and me were different. We belonged in the school playcage or out on the scam round the Loop, and Crystal needed her Tango to be a grown-up, like she'd never needed anything so much before.

I missed the grand exit because I had to get the last bus from the depot, late-night buses being few and far between round the Loop, and Somerton a long way away. It appears that Mrs Teresa O'Leary herded Crystal home from the San Marino that night thinking she had won, because Crystal had never ever dared cross her before. But she reckoned without Tango.

Tango loved Crystal. He desperately wanted Crystal to have the child so that she would be his baby's mammy. Tango meant to look after Crystal, and his baby. He wanted that more than anything else in the world. He didn't mouth about it in the San Marino, because he knew that nothing that was said or done that night was going to make any difference.

Action, not words. Poor old Tango never was good with words. Tango's plan didn't resolve any of their long-term problems. Tango wasn't programmed to think long term, so the idea of a long-term resolution was too much to expect. What Tango's plan did was to buy the two lovers a little happiness for a short time.

I am glad it worked out that way, for their sake.

CHAPTER
SIX

Mrs Teresa O'Leary set out to arrange getting rid of the baby, for Crystal's own good, she kept insisting, because Crystal was just a child herself still and it would ruin her life.

"She didn't give a thumb what happened to Tango or Crystal," Madonna maintains. "If Manus had broken Tango's back and got away with it, his loving mother wouldn't have been one bit worried."

"You think of somebody else for a change," Mrs O scolded Crystal. "What will it do to your poor brother Manus if he gets in any more trouble?"

Getting rid of the baby was never going to be straightforward, because their doctor is Doctor Graham at the Loop Centre, and he is a stickler for the book. If Mrs O had tried to put Crystal in on the usual NHS system, questions would have been asked about the under-age bit, and the word might have got to the cops. It isn't that difficult to arrange a way round that, there are doctors and doctors, but most of them are not the sort Mrs O would have come across on her journey through life.

"I don't know any," Funny Bum lied to her.

She knew Tango and Crystal were both dead set against having an abortion, and she wasn't going to help. I've also heard hints that Funny Bum funded Tango's plan, but that may be based on what happened later. The same story has been told about Hank. It could have been either, or neither, or both.

Anyway, Tango must have got the funds he needed somewhere. The bit of the plan he had left to fix was transport for Crystal and himself.

It may have been force of habit, but he recruited Jackie Coney to help, though he didn't tell Jackie what he was really up to.

"He kept saying he wanted a real flash motor. He was fussed about it, but he never said what for," Jackie told me, with the implication that if Jackie had known what for, he wouldn't have bothered himself. He'd have skived off.

Anyway, Tango ding-donged the door of Jackie's place and off they went to get a car, over Beltown.

Tango passed up three or four nice autos that would have done them any other day, when it was just a question of a ride around the flats, which is all it usually was. Joyriding had been a game with those two, from year dot. Tango liked anything to do with cars, and Jackie was in it for the thrill.

"Silly buggers!" Melons says. "You've got to be careful what you get into with Jackie, but I don't think they ever did it for profit. Pinching cars for a living was too organized for Tango. You know that, Chris. Anyway, if Tango was doing it, he'd have had a lot more money, wouldn't he?"

Melons always was ambivalent about Jackie, for much the same reasons I was. Jackie was our mate, but you can only take being a mate so far. Some of Jackie's stuff was better kept out of.

"We just used to take them for laughs!" is Jackie's version, and by and large it is probably true.

Tango picked a flash scarlet BMW two-seater from outside the Ali Khazan, and off they went, vroom-vroom and two-wheeling round corners, scaring old dears. All their usual form.

They dumped it down the back of the Oil Yard, about twenty minutes later, and cut over to the flats.

Tango said he was headed for Funny Bum's flat to see her about something, and Jackie Coney went off to do whatever Jackie Coneys do. He says there was never a word to suggest that this time was any different from the others. Of course, Jackie didn't know that Crystal was having a baby at that stage, so he wasn't on the look-out for anything. That's what Jackie says.

Tango didn't go to Funny Bum's flat.

Instead he must have doubled back, picked up the scarlet BMW and headed for his rendezvous with Crystal O'Leary, after school.

Nobody saw them meet. It could have been anywhere.

Off they drove in the BMW, Tango in his NHS glasses stuck together with Sellotape and Crystal in her schoolgirl outfit, complete with schoolbag and geography homework and a just-beginning-to-be-noticeable baby bump, her hair pulled tight back, held by an elastic band with a blue bobble.

It sounds so weird that it must be true; they had a kind of honeymoon. He took her shopping and they got her honeymoon clothes, so she wouldn't stand out in her school uniform.

Then they booked into a hotel for two nights. Despite their obvious youth, nobody asked any questions, so I'm left wondering about the hotel.

"It was lovely," Crystal told Madonna later. "There was a kettle in the room so we could have our own tea and bikkies, and we got more the second day, though they didn't bring us any the day we were leaving."

It was some seaside place. They went walking on the prom, and she did look-out while he pulled her some flowers from one of the displays.

"I was in bed, and he had this pansy in his teeth!" Crystal said, with a giggle. "He's bouncing round the room doing a Spanish act with two Diet Coke tins for castanets and I've got the giggles and I'm worried because he's banging the floor with his heels, and he'll bring the ceiling down on the people below. 'For you', he says, and he gives me the pansy. 'What am I going to do with this?' I ask him, looking at my pansy, and he opens his big mouth and eats it!"

"Not big or posh but *very* nice," is Crystal's well-satisfied verdict on the hotel. They didn't eat in the dining-room after the first night, because of the money. They smuggled in take-aways. "Only Brian dropped this vindaloo in the lift and we're trying to get it back in the tray and we're going up and down and up and down and up and down so nobody else will get in and see!" Crystal was all sparkly about it.

Tango and Crystal got away with it in their honeymoon hotel, a case of fortune favouring the desperate. Then they moved on. Apparently Tango *had* a plan, it wasn't just talk, which shows how important it was to him getting things right for Crystal, even if the plan was a Tango-wonky one.

"It's a surprise!" he told Crystal, and they headed off in their car. "Everything's worked out, like. You're not to worry because I'm looking after you now and there's no Manus to be afraid of, and your old mum can keep her snout out." Crystal thought it was good. He had taken away her terrors. Her Brian was going to protect her from everything.

The car turned up four days later and two hundred miles away in a lay-by. They had managed to break a wing mirror, and the packaging from two fried burger suppers was all over the floor, but otherwise it was unharmed, though someone had unwound a Nina Simone tape for no apparent reason and wrapped it round the gear lever.

The birds had flown.

Consternation ... but not widespread consternation.

Mrs Teresa O'Leary didn't let a squeak out of her. She sat tight and hoped her little boy's problems were over, because if Manus couldn't find Tango he couldn't maim him, could he? Goodness knows what story she fobbed off Evett with, Crystal being still due in for her lessons, but nobody seems to have picked up on it until much later.

On the Tangello side of the wire, Auntie Florence Tangello wasn't put out. Tango had dutifully fixed things up for Grannie T. He had Funny Bum Johnston calling in to check up twice a day. That is just like Funny Bum. In one of her modes she is a One-Woman Welfare System for the whole of Buffey's Loop Estate. I have heard it offered as a plea in mitigation by her Social Worker.

Crystal, gone. Tango, gone.

Gone where?

Tango's surprise was that they were going out with a travelling fair, and they were going to live in one of the wagons, and be happy ever after.

"Hank knew Mr Porter that ran it," Crystal told Madonna. "Brian helped out with the motors, and I did the darts. It was the yellow wagon we were squeezed into, with our duvet in between the boxes where they keep the prizes.

"Sometimes Brian was like a baby," she said. "My big gentle baby. And I liked it, because he'd done all he could to look after me and make things right for me, got us a job and somewhere we could be together even if it was just an old wagon, and now I was looking after him. Only I didn't realize then that that was the way it would always be."

Tango had solved their accommodation problem and got them some money to live on, without the interference from officialdom Crystal feared and expected. Crystal was very impressed. She must have known somewhere inside herself that it couldn't last, but she was so taken up with him then that it didn't matter. Of course, Tango's problem-solving technique ties in with his short termism – the season for travelling fairs is only summer-long. I suppose one summer of bliss is better than no summer at all.

Funny Bum remained as their only contact with the Loop, although she is a bit evasive about it, but she always knew how to contact Tango if she needed to.

When the season stopped the problems should have begun, but it didn't turn out that way. Housing could have been a bother, but it wasn't to Tango.

They were left in a small seaside town called Cowley Bay. About three miles out of it along the coast there is a place called Palkirk. There is nothing to Palkirk but a dismal line of little 1930s beach chalets. They are locked up to rot a bit more all winter, because who wants to freeze in a one-room wooden chalet with the North Sea crashing at the door? The huts are not designed to protect their inhabitants from the elements.

Equally, they aren't designed to keep out somebody like Tango, operating on the principle that there is very little reason why anybody like Tango would want to get in. Padlocked metal windows and doors are about the height of it, and most of the owners don't even bother with that, making do with bolts and Yale.

Tango apparently worked his way through half a dozen, collecting the bits and pieces of their scanty furnishings that appealed to Crystal, and set up house in the best chalet he could find, which had "San Lorenzo" on the door. Maybe it was an echo of the San Marino that made him pick it, or maybe there were fewer rust holes in the roof.

The camping stove I can understand: it is the kind of thing people do leave behind in beach huts, ditto the sleeping bags they used as a coverlet, and the beach lilos that were their mattress; but the two fur coats defeat me. They were old and moth eaten, but how had they got left behind in the first place? Who trips across twenty yards of shingle to the North Sea in an old fur coat?

Apparently, Crystal and Tango wrapped the two fur coats round themselves when they were sitting beside the camping stove at night.

They also wore them when they were having their idyllic moments, walking up and down by the edge of the silvery sea, their bare feet sinking in the shingle.

I forget what you call it when the sea has a line of light along the spines of the waves as they break on the stones – phosphorence? I think we learned about that at William Whitlaw, I got it somewhere anyway. I doubt if Tango tried to explain it to Crystal, and I equally doubt if she wanted to know.

Maybe it was only the one night, but according to Madonna that is Crystal's abiding memory.

"Brian tore some planks off the back of one of the chalets, and we had this bonfire that night," Crystal told Madonna. "The fire was crackling red and all, and we snuggled up beside it in the old coats. '*Love you,*' he says. '*Love you too,*' I told him, and we just snuggled there."

Fire flames flickering on the shingle, red embers and the cold dark blue of the water stretching out into the bay as far as they could see, the clean fresh smell of the sea and the smoke, snuggling down with their beer cans, and the baby inside stirring when Tango laid his head on Crystal's lap. The most important thing was being alone with each other and their about-to-be little one. No mummies or daddies or aunties or grannies or social workers or Sam-Sams or Evetts or cops or attendance men, because they'd walked out on that world.

They were alone together. All they needed, they had. That memory is what Crystal came back to again and again.

"I really did love Brian then," Crystal told

Madonna. It was as simple as that, and why shouldn't it be? To the world Tango was a bust-case, but not in Crystal's eyes.

"I'd have done anything he wanted," she told Madonna. "Gone anywhere he said. Nothing else mattered to me but being with him. My big, funny, gentle Brian, with his stupid grin and his silly Tango-walk and his wonky glasses! I just knew we were all right so long as we stuck together."

She said it, and she meant it … then.

It is good and right that they had that one sweet time together before it all went wrong – and it was going to go wrong. It wasn't going to come out all hearts and flowers and baby bootees for Crystal and Tango and their baby, and little Crystal *must* have begun to suspect that it wouldn't, because she wasn't born stupid.

CHAPTER SEVEN

Enter the Major. An ancient ex-Army dentist, he carried himself like a tin soldier, and called Funny Bum Johnston "Bunny" when he was in an affectionate mood. His hearing aid may have been dicky, or perhaps he simply misheard her name in the buzz at the Builders' Arms. The broken down Major was fond of Funny Bum, and he was a romantic. He had false teeth, lower and upper (so much for his dentistry), NHS bifocals, and gammy innards that were kept going by a little battery-operated machine, programmed to flash on and off so his fellow drinkers would know that he was dead and not just sitting still waiting for someone to buy him one.

The big deal about the Major was that he had a beat up, rusty Ford Orion, which he kept taxed and on the road by virtue of hardly ever moving it any further than the pub and back.

The poor old Major believed his finest hour had

come when Funny Bum arrived in the Builders'
Arms in a flurry of cheap scent, and told him he
was taking her to Palkirk and she was paying for
the petrol.

"My pleasure, Bunny," smiled the geriatric
Major, and he straightened his teeth and headed
for the door, with Funny Bum in tow, carrying
his fags.

It wasn't a pleasure trip for Funny Bum. She
needed to speak to Tango urgently, because of
dramatic developments in Tangello Land, where
Auntie Flo had taken the hump and dumped
Grannie Tangello and her wheelchair out on the
street, greatly to Funny Bum's consternation.

They survived the journey unscathed, but the
walk along the beach at Palkirk almost did for the
Major. The wind blew the rain in their faces and
waves raged up the beach, seagulls wheeled and
squealed over their heads.

"The things I do for friends!" Funny Bum muttered, grabbing the Major by the arm to keep him
upright.

"Can't say I remember who young Tangello is,"
said the Major.

"You're not missing much, Major, believe me,"
Funny Bum said bitterly.

The Major began to falter. One or two bigger
puffs and she thought he might blow away.
Halfway along the beach, he had to stop and
fiddle with his NHS life support machinery,
plopping down wheezily on the breezeblock

wall outside one of the beach huts.

He had a little red light attached to a wire that ran down the inside of his shirt, appearing at his wrist beside his watch strap. The red light started to blink, and there was a humming sound.

"What's up, Major?" from Funny Bum.

"Blessed machine," muttered the Major, gone red in the face.

A long fumble through his pockets followed, a vain search for batteries.

In the end, Funny Bum had to totter back to the car to locate the spare pack which he carried with him at all times, except that he had forgotten to pocket them – no doubt muddled by the excitement of his away-day with Bunny. Now Funny Bum is not a natural seasider: she was in a short red miniskirt and a black velveteen jacket, with high, high, high-heeled red shoes, and tights with silver butterflies fluttering up her thighs.

"I wanted to look like a lady," she says. "The Major appreciated things like that, poor old bugger." The red shoes had made progress along the beach erratic, and now that she found herself on an emergency sprint back to the car, they had to come off.

"It was my poor feet, or him conking out on me!" she says.

She located the batteries, and started back.

All those beach huts look much the same and, bending against the wind and the rain, Funny Bum became acutely aware that there was no sign of the Major on the strip where she felt sure she had left him.

Panic stations!

"Major!" she was yelling, running up and down and trying to make herself heard against the roar of the waves. She got very damp and frightened, and didn't know what to do, so she ran for help.

The by-now-very-noticeably-pregnant Crystal was taking a lie-down in their love-hut, but Tango had been busy. He had plastic flowers on the table, the camping stove lit and the duvets laid round the edge of the floor, where the draught blew up from underneath. Apparently the walls of the beach hut didn't quite meet up with the floor. Funny Bum says you could get your fingers right down the gap.

Bang-bang on the door. "Hi, it's me. Help me!" gasped Funny Bum. "Something awful's happened to the Major."

All three of them, Crystal included, set off in the driving rain and wind.

Not a sign. Not a sausage. No Major.

"Oh, shit! He'll die! I'll have to tell his wife!" said Funny Bum.

I forgot to mention the Major's wife. That is partly because she was more or less invisible, as far as the people who knew the Major went. She had arthritis. Mrs the Major was seldom seen outside their three-room basement flat.

"His bloody pension dies with him!" Funny Bum was insisting, though I don't think that can be right. I think she was contemplating having to keep Mrs the Major in funds because she had mislaid the poor Major.

They were up and down the row, in and out of the beach houses and the rabbit hutches and the garden sheds, searching along the scrubland at the back.

"Get a car! Get the police!" Funny Bum was insisting.

"*We* can't get the police!" Crystal wailed.

She was wrapped up in the mouldy fur coat with an old duvet over her shoulders and a pair of yellow Paddington boots on her feet. The boots must have been lifted from one of the sea-front shops in Cowley Bay during one of their shopping trips for macaroni. Apparently, Crystal's pregnancy had got her onto macaroni and they couldn't keep lifting macaroni from the one supermarket there was without attracting notice. Some of the macaroni had to be bought, which must have cut a swathe through their finances. At one point she was on at least two packets a day, dowsed in strawberry jam.

"We *have* to get the police!" from Funny Bum.

"*You* get them then!" from Crystal, brutally realistic. "We'll clear off or something, till they're done."

It says something for Tango that he reacted differently to Funny Bum's very real distress. For once he completely ignored Crystal, beyond telling her to get back to the beach hut and look after herself. He should never have let her out in the wet in the first place, in her condition, but they were all in such a state about the Major that they hadn't thought – which is plain mad as usual, but then they lived their whole lives that way, nothing was commonplace reasonable.

"You get Crystal clear. I'll get the cops," from Tango.

Tango, *getting the cops*? Tango with his long history of minor lawlessness? Well, Funny Bum was in tears, and Tango was upset about it and couldn't think of any other way to help. He owed Funny Bum a bundle for looking after the other woman in his life, his gran. Tango always was loyal to people he cared for: Crystal, Funny Bum, his gran, even Jackie Coney, though I think his loyalty was misplaced in that case.

The contrast with Crystal speaks for itself.

Funny Bum and a nose-out-of-joint Crystal struggled back through the gale to the beach hut. Crystal was really really upset and angry with Funny Bum. It was only when they were in the hut that Funny Bum discovered she still had the Major's car keys in her pocket.

"Oh, well, my Brian can start any car he wants to!" from Crystal, through chattering teeth. She said it with some pride.

The trouble was that Tango didn't go for the Major's car. He wouldn't have known which car it was, anyway. It hadn't occurred to Funny Bum to tell him, because *she* knew, and anyway there was only the one car parked at the end of Beach

Road. But Tango didn't go that way. He headed for the nearest car he could find, nipping round the back of the beach huts, through the scrub, over the barbed wire fence and down the eighteenth hole to the golf course car park. There he could have stopped, thought, and gone in to summon help from the members, or simply asked if he could make a phone call – but that was too simple for Tango. Or maybe the golf club was an institution so far out of his mind-set that he couldn't bring himself to go inside.

Which is how he came to get himself lifted trying to start a car which was parked up against the MEMBERS ONLY sign. It was a Bentley, which is why Tango went for it instead of one of the others. Why pinch a mini, after all? Take your pick from the best. It also turned out to be the one with the loudest alarm system.

Tango ignored the racket and struggled to start the car, so he was nicked by a quorum of outraged members.

"There's an old man down on the beach and his heart thing's gone phut!" Tango tried telling them, but they didn't believe him. He kept on telling them, becoming very emotional about it, and then two cops appeared in a car.

More from Tango, nearly in tears by this time.

In the end Tango, the two policemen and two club members set off to search for the Major, just in case Tango was telling the truth.

They hunted up and down the beach and sure

enough, there was the Major, huddled down in a gorse bush, where he'd collapsed.

Tango, the two policemen and one of the golfers staggered across the eighteenth hole with the Major on an old piece of corrugated iron as a makeshift stretcher. The Major was laid out in the clubhouse, an ambulance on the way.

Tango went to the bog.

Maybe it was force of William Whitlaw habit, born of his breakout school days, but being allowed to relieve himself unaccompanied by the cops was too much for Tango. Any one of his old mates at William Whitlaw could have told the cops what would happen – not that people ever did tell on Tango, much. Melons says the strength of Tango's old I-don't-bust-on-my-mates thing rubbed off on the rest of us ... though *maybe* not on Myrtle, but who knows?

Out the window, and away.

He didn't head for the chalet because, in the course of his attempts to get them going about the Major, the truth about forced entrance at the chalet had been revealed. He thought he was the one who was in trouble, and if he wasn't there, nothing much could be pinned on Crystal.

The cops arrived in front of the chalet as Crystal went out the back. The cops lifted Funny Bum and that left Crystal hiding out on a sand bank, draped in the duvet.

It was a real downer for the cops. They had nothing to hold Funny Bum on and they knew it.

Their one real hope of putting anyone away was Tango, and Tango had bugged off.

What happened next must have been something like this. Seven months pregnant, wet to the skin and wrapped up in a soaked and gorse-ripped duvet, shivering alone in a bus shelter on the sea-front at Cowley, Crystal made up her mind that there was only one thing she could do, which shows how desperate she must have been. She decided to go straight home to her mum.

Tango, hunting, would have found her.

"I've got to go home, Brian," from Crystal. "You've got to let me, because of our baby. I can't have our baby like this."

They'd be shivering in some beach shelter, clinging together. He must have had some inkling that his good time was over, but Crystal *knew*.

Brutally, that is what it came down to.

"I'm sure Crystal took over the decision making then," Madonna insists. "Just as well, too. I don't blame her. She did it because she had to. If it meant hurting Tango's self image as her provider then she was going to do it, because it had to be done. She was near her time. She hoped she could manage Manus, and she knew she couldn't sit it out and give birth in some bloody chalet with the wind blowing through the floorboards. She did the right thing."

"Yeah," I said. "But looking after Crystal by himself was Tango's big number, and he had been doing it, against all the odds. How could she take that off him?"

"You really don't like Crystal, do you, Chris?" she said. "I'll tell you something. I'd have done it like a shot."

"You'd never have been mixed up with him in the first place, Donna!" I said.

"If I *had* been I'd have made damn sure he didn't waste his condom on a gerbil!" she said. "Look, I'm sorry for Tango, but I'm not blaming Crystal. Somebody had to sort it out. She loved him, but she had to be sensible."

"It must have been a real king-sized downer for the big guy," I said.

"Too bad," she said. "Too bad he never grew up."

CHAPTER EIGHT

"It's my baby, and I'm having it," defiantly, from Crystal. "I'm too far gone. You can't touch my baby now."

"Oh, glory be to God!" from Mrs O. "Would you listen to the child?"

"I'll kill that bastard Tangello when I lay hands on him!" Manus spouted.

Manus was back, out of a job, drinking again, and looping the Loop like a wolf, sniffing for Tango's blood.

"You leave my Brian alone, Manus!" from Crystal, in tears. "Do you hear me, Manus? Don't you dare lay a finger on Brian!"

"We'll see about that, you stupid little bitch!" from Manus. "If Tangello turns up sniffing after you I'll lay more than a finger on him. I'll break the bugger's back."

"Brian won't come here," Crystal said. "*You* made sure of that. And I hope you're proud of yourself, Manus O'Leary!"

That about sums up Crystal's homecoming.

Still, little Crystal was home safe, waddling round the house balloon big, with her mother fussing after her. She had held out against her mother, and Tango, and taken her own course.

That is not to say that Crystal had dumped Tango, far from it. She loved him and needed him, and she knew she was going to need him even more when the baby was born. She'd worked out with him that she would stay home with Mother, warm and comfortable with her feet up, until then. Tango would steer clear of the house, Crystal's story to her family being that Tango had run off and dumped her. The fall-back position was that if Manus turned nasty and tried to beat her, Tango was going to have Crystal out of it. He was quite determined about that. But Tango needed Crystal more than she needed him, that is the truth of it.

He needed to be near her.

He came back to Buffey's Loop. That is, he was *reported* as back, about the place, but he never showed up at the San Marino or any of his usual haunts. Jackie Coney and Melons heard rumours that he'd been seen, notably around the time of Stevie Bakuli's funeral, but they swear they never saw him. Myrtle and Madonna were no better, which shows just how determined and single-minded Tango must have been.

Mrs O had roped in the Geek and Sister Monica Rose to help. Sister appeared in Mrs O's house every day and read Crystal little moral lectures, with prayer sessions in between.

Crystal told Madonna that Sister was weird, but she put up with it because Mrs O was relying on Sister so much by that time.

"She tried to take over everything about my baby," Crystal said. "That's in between preaching at me, and trying to get the Geek to pass his hands over me. Not kinky stuff. Religious stuff. Like there was bad in me that had to be got out. I mean she was trying to help, but it was all tied up with mumbo-jumbo. I put up with it, because of Mum. The Geek acted like he was God's forgiving messenger, and I was a sinning sister he had to get back to the fold. Mum and them were going to do all the benefit stuff for me, but I said 'No'. I got the Welfare lady to help me and I went and did all the signing up myself, puff-puff down the road. Fixed up the Welfare and my Giro and everything."

This is interesting in two ways: one, it confirms that little Crystal had got herself a dose of confidence from having defied her mother's edict about getting rid of the baby, and maybe from the realization that she was going to have to cope with some of the things Tango plainly wasn't up to coping with; two, and more important, was the stroke she pulled in her dealings over the Giro, but that didn't emerge until later. It was a manoeuvre the old Crystal of the Goody Club would never have seemed capable of. Crystal was growing up fast, certainly faster than old Tango.

Meanwhile, Manus was on slow boil. Sister Monica Rose was doing what she could to help Mrs O cope with him, sending the Geek to pull Manus out of pubs on the day he got his money, but she couldn't cover everything.

"Manus was out of control, wasn't he?" Jackie Coney says, and that about sums it up, although Manus never went beyond the verbals with Crystal.

"It was seeing her sitting there nursing her bump, I think," Madonna says. "Primitive masculine thing. He'd fisted her when she was just Crystal, but now she was different, transformed. Crystal told me she felt safe enough in the house with Manus, despite everything. She was fairly convinced he would stick to the mouthing, at least till the baby was born. As the plan seems to have been that they'd get the baby safely born and then do another runner, baby and all, that was what mattered to Crystal at the time."

The places he could be expected to be, Tango generally wasn't, but every so often someone would report a sighting, which would set Manus off again.

Manus got it into his head that Tango was spending the nights at his Auntie Flo Tangello's. He stormed down to Auntie Flo's house, but he drew a blank.

"He's not here, and if he turns up he's not getting in the door!" Auntie Flo said. She was still in the middle of her strung out drama over the grannie. Auntie Flo's version of the ejection of Grannie T was this: Funny Bum had turned up on Grannie's birthday; Funny Bum and Grannie had a celebration and Funny Bum got the old lady drunk; there were complications afterwards with Grannie's bowels and she had to go into hospital and be stomach pumped. Auntie Flo got the Welfare on her neck for not looking after the old lady and Auntie Flo turned brutal and said it wasn't her responsibility anyway, and she wasn't having Grannie back from the hospital.

That is how Tango's grannie ended up in Funny Bum's flat. Tango sneaked round and visited his grannie early every morning, without fail. He'd sit there and hold her hand and read her bits out of the *Sun*. It was all top security stuff, because Funny Bum drew the line at having Manus landing on her doorstep.

"He never missed a day," Funny Bum says admiringly. "He really doted on the old lady and did everything he could for her. She was nuts about him. He was so good and gentle with her. When he was there, he wouldn't even let me do the nursing things. He was going to do them. It mattered to them both that he did those things. And he was always bringing her little presents that he thought she'd like – and of course she *always* liked them, because they came from him. He was really wrapped up in the old lady."

So Auntie Flo had washed her hands of Tango and Grannie T, but of course that wasn't much help to her, confronted by a half-cut Manus cursing her nephew on her doorstep.

"Brian's cleared off, and I never want to see him again," Auntie Flo told him.

True to form, Manus didn't believe Auntie Flo. She slammed the door on him and he broke the kitchen window and rampaged through the house.

Auntie Flo called the cops. Calling the cops is one of the things that just isn't done round the Flats, but Manus carried on so badly that he put Auntie Flo in fear of her life.

Manus was lifted, drunk and disorderly, another score in his mind against Tango.

They held him for two hours and then they had to let him go because there was no room in the cells. So they told him, "Go near that woman again and you are nicked for ever," and set him out on the streets, supposedly sobered up, *before* closing time.

Five pints later, and Manus was loose on the estate, ranting and raving, on the hunt for Tango.

Funny Bum got her windows done but, unlike Auntie Flo, Funny Bum did not call the cops. She just got a hammer and nails and boarded things up, and then she coped with Grannie T, who was having hysterics.

Manus staggered home at dawn, after the Geek had picked him up down by the canal, threatening to throw himself in. He was half dragged, half carted home, draped on the Geek's shoulder.

The Geek heaved Manus into the house and put him to bed.

As Manus was being led in through the front door, Tango was bundling out of the window of Crystal's little pink-and-white rabbit wallpapered room.

"I wanted Brian with me," Crystal said. "It was me that made him come and spend the nights there, though he wanted to as well. I had to know he still loved me, despite me being big and all."

So that solves where Tango was spending the nights while Manus was out hunting him.

They had it worked out to a fine art. Mrs O would go off to her soup kitchen prayer sessions with Sister and the Geek, and Manus would go off to Tango hunt. When the coast was clear, Tango would leave the Milkwhite Bread container at Hank's. He'd slip up the canal bank past their love seat and over the fence at the back of Mrs O's little house in Stanley Street, into the yard, through the back window, up to Crystal's room and into bed, cradling his big head against the warmth of his child in her swollen belly.

That's why nobody was able to pinpoint where Tango was hanging out. He was spending the nights with Crystal until just before dawn, when he got out through the window again and went on his pilgrimage to his grannie in Funny Bum's flat. During the day he helped out with odd jobs round the back at Hank's, where no one could see him.

That's how it was for a while.

Then one evening Mrs O arrived home very late after helping the Geek bed down some of the winos under the viaduct and she heard funny noises. She took it into her head that they were coming from Crystal's room at the back, over the kitchen. She turned off the gas under the kettle and rushed upstairs, heart-scared that Manus had got over his hang-up about not touching Crystal.

In she barged yelling, "Manus! Stop it!"

Tango and Crystal were in bed.

Mrs O went up the wall.

"Get out! Get out you wicked git!" she was screaming.

Next thing, Manus appeared, wakened from a drunken stupor by the yells coming from his mother.

All hell let loose!

Tango, in his underpants, headed for his usual "door", the window. He got through it onto the roof of the kitchen, with Manus coming after him, clawing through the window yelling and cursing and Mrs O wailing and weeping and scolding and trying to hold Manus back. Crystal was having hysterics.

Tango landed in the yard and made for the back wall and the relative safety of the canal bank.

Manus blundered after him. He put his weight on the roof and his foot went through it and the jagged edge of the tin cut into the back of his leg, just above the calf. He needed eighteen stitches.

Tango shivered all the way back to the Milk-white Bread container in his Y-fronts.

Manus hopped round the yard awash with blood.

Mrs O wept on the bed.

"Mum! Mum! Help me. The baby's started!" Crystal cried as her waters broke.

CHAPTER NINE

Tango's baby was born three weeks prematurely, weighing in at six pounds and one ounce. Dominic Cosmo O'Leary had big hands and big feet like his daddy.

He was called Dominic because Crystal liked the name, Cosmo after Mrs O'Leary's Uncle Cosmo back in Cork. No input on name from Tango's side, you'll notice.

"Tango was so chuffed that he didn't care, so long as the baby and Crystal were all right," Madonna says, and after the initial scare, they were.

"My Brian made a real fuss of me!" Crystal told her proudly. "Flowers and fruit and everything and Hank had to come with him and see my baby. Brian was all red in the face and dancing about with excitement. Hank put some notes on my pillow when he was going out, in an envelope, so we could get stuff for the baby. Then he took Brian off and they both got plastered, which shows how off the wall my Brian was, because he doesn't hardly ever drink. They ended up back in Hank's house with Brian telling Mrs Hank how he'd never been so happy in his life, and what a great daddy he was going to be."

The birth of Tango's baby can't have been exactly happy hour at the O'Learys', but it signified a win for Crystal. After all, Crystal had *had* her baby.

Meanwhile Sam-Sam had got himself implicated. It happened after Stevie Bakuli's funeral, a bit before Baby D was born. Stevie Bakuli being dead is a key development in Tango's story. Stevie jumped off a warehouse roof three days after Crystal arrived back at Mrs O's. He was killed instantly, impaling himself on the railings round the warehouse yard. It was very messy.

Of course, everyone round Buffey's Loop knew the cops were to blame. They shouldn't have disturbed him with his little can of petrol when all he was trying to do was burn the place down. It wasn't done for an insurance scam or anything logical like that. Stevie Bakuli just liked the noise fire engines make.

At the back of the crowd at Stevie's funeral was Sam-Sam, representing the William Whitlaw School. Evett had sent him in his best suit. Sam-Sam was intent on showing there was no ill feeling towards the dead, despite the fact that Stevie had won fame head-butting him in the playcage, spreading Sam-Sam's nose and busting the frame of his glasses.

With Stevie safely buried, everyone went off to the Builders' Arms to think of semi-positive things to say about him, which didn't come easy to some.

Including Sam-Sam.

Sam-Sam and his Guinness were perched in the corner consoling each other when in rolled Funny Bum Johnston. She was all in black, and crying. Funny Bum is like that at funerals.

Funny Bum cornered Sam-Sam and his Guinness.

"He thinks a lot of you, Mr Samuelson, Tango does," Funny Bum told Sam-Sam. "That's why I thought you ought to know."

"Know what?" said Sam-Sam, little guessing what he was getting himself into.

"Well, it's his old grannie," Funny Bum said. "You know how Tango feels about her. Now his Auntie Flo has chucked his grannie out, and she is living in my flat, only the Welfare are after me, and I can't have her there for ever, poor old dear."

"That's terrible," Sam-Sam said, genuinely concerned, because he is a genuine guy.

"She needs a commode thing and it is in Tango's house, but the auntie won't let us have it and I can't have another off the Welfare because there's already one allocated," Funny Bum complained.

"Well, tell Tango to fetch it!" Sam-Sam said.

"He's gone walkies, hasn't he?" Funny Bum said, lying in her teeth. "I think you ought to do something. You're his teacher."

"*Was* his teacher," said Sam-Sam, backing off, not unreasonably in my view, considering that Tango was hardly ever there to be taught anyway.

Funny Bum has her head screwed on. She knew Sam-Sam was the man she needed, an ex-Labour councillor with an in where it counts, so she went for it.

"You don't want an old woman's death on your conscience, do you, Mr Samuelson?" Funny Bun demanded. "What are you going to do about it?"

Nothing was Sam-Sam's reaction, but his social conscience forced him to say something consoling, so he said he would have a word about the commode with the Welfare in his official capacity as Deputy Head of William Whitlaw.

"Well, I hope you do!" Funny Bum said, and she went off and left him.

Next morning Sam-Sam got on to the Welfare, because he had told Funny Bum that he would. That goes to show the sort of guy Sam-Sam was – soft hearted. It was why he would never have made Head Warder. Evett would have kept out of it.

Sam-Sam reported the auntie to the Big Boots at the Welfare, for holding on to Grannie T's commode.

Louise Brennan from the Welfare came up trumps. She sent someone round to take the commode from Auntie Flo who had normal bowels and no need of it, but after that the Rule Book caught up with Louise. The Big Boots told Louise that the Rule Book said she had to re-allocate the commode to the next one on their list. Grannie Tangello was deemed to have given it up voluntarily, and she had to go to the bottom of the list of starters, which is eight months long. She was somewhat discommoded, to quote Sam-Sam.

Auntie Flo raged down to William Whitlaw on her day off to complain about losing the commode, which she regarded as her personal property. She would have hauled Sam-Sam out, except that Evett came to Sam-Sam's rescue, no doubt with some malicious glee. Evett and Sam-Sam never did get on, and now she had another hold on him.

I don't know the rest of that story, but one thing was established: Sam-Sam was linked in Louise Brennan's mind with the business of caring for Tango's grannie.

Being Sam-Sam, he took it on board. He began to feel responsible for Tango's grannie having a rough time.

Sam-Sam fought her corner with the Welfare and actually got her a Community Care Nurse calling at Funny Bum's twice a week which, with the state of the Welfare in our place, is the equivalent of winning the pools.

Then he set out to locate Tango, because he knew the Community Care Nurse wouldn't last the next set of cuts, because they never do. Of course, Funny Bum could have put him in touch with Tango easily enough, but she wasn't going to.

Sam-Sam was barging around the place trying to track Tango down, while Manus was on the same mission, but neither one knew of the activities of the other.

Sam-Sam's detective work meant that he heard a bit of the Crystal story – the running-off-with-Tango bit – and he heard she was back around the Loop, so he decided he would give his ex-pupil a call, in the hope that she would know where Tango was.

He was greeted by a determined Crystal clutching a little baby to her breast.

"Crystal!" he said.

"Mr Samuelson," she said. Crystal was always respectful to Sam-Sam at school, and she hadn't dropped the habit.

"Is that yours?" he blurted out.

"Yeah. Lovely, isn't he?" she said, and she added proudly, "I'm the first in our year that's had one."

Long pause from Sam-Sam.

"Well, congratulations, Crystal," he managed.

"I'm well pleased," Crystal said.

Sam-Sam didn't want to quiz her too much, because he didn't know the score, so he veered off and launched into Funny Bum's story, which of course she knew all about anyway, but she wasn't letting on that she did.

"Do you know where Brian Tangello is?"

"Me? No. Why would I?" from Crystal, a little defiantly.

Of course she was clasping what Sam-Sam guessed was Tango's baby, and he felt he had to be tactful.

"Well, I thought..." he said, looking hard at the baby which, he says, was a wriggly little bundle.

"I don't know nothing about old Brian, Mr Samuelson," Crystal said. Of course it was a bare-faced lie. If she had told the truth and got Sam-Sam on her side he might have been able to do something for her as he'd done for Grannie T; got her a flat or something, by using his contacts.

"She knew where her big boyfriend was all right," Sam-Sam says. "But she wasn't telling me. She was tough as teak about it."

Don't bugger about in my life, Mr Samuelson. I'm not in your maths class now was the not very subliminal message she gave him; this from the little white mouse he was used to seeing at the back of the class.

The truth is that Crystal had pulled her stroke with the Welfare, getting her Giro, and now she was doing all she could to back up her story, so she wasn't going to admit knowing anything about Tango.

This is the score: when Crystal arrived back in Stanley Street from the beach hut she was under immediate pressure. The Welfare were after her to name the father of her child, and she was afraid to name Tango in case he might go to prison.

Then she heard Stevie was dead, so she told the Welfare it was Stevie's baby.

"I didn't think anyone would be bothered after that," Crystal later told Madonna, tearfully.

"Stevie was pronged dead on the railings, wasn't he? He was out of it for sure."

Well, she was wrong.

CHAPTER
TEN

"Of course I didn't tell Brian," Crystal said to Madonna long afterwards. "Why should I? It was only between me and the Welfare. Anyway, he was dead keen on being a daddy, and I knew he wouldn't like it. So I kept my mouth shut. I never told nobody."

So naturally enough nobody knew. Mrs O and Manus must have presumed that Crystal had done the right thing and informed on Tango – this being *before* the night the waters broke – because the Giros started arriving after her interview with the Welfare.

So nobody knew about dead Stevie being a daddy but Crystal and the Welfare. That's the way Crystal believed it to be, in her little dream world, while in the *real* world, administrative wheels had started clicking, because that is what happens when buttons get pressed and names go down in Big Daddy Books.

Click-click-click, catching up on Crystal's life.

The pay-off wasn't long coming but, although it was down to the intervention of the Welfare, it didn't come from Louise Brennan or the Big Boots.

The clicks resulting from Crystal's stroke caught up with Tango when he was out on a typical Buffey's Loop Mission of Mercy, helping Grannie T.

It was three o'clock in the morning, and Tango was wheeling one of those big old prams round the Loop, on his way to Funny Bum's flat. On the pram was a camper's portaloo, a plastic bucket-in-a-frame job, which Tango had bought from a man for a few pounds.

It was another present from Tango to his grannie, no doubt funded by a soft hearted Hank. The portaloo was, not the pram. His grannie had no need of a pram, being permanently stuck in her chair. I don't know where he got the pram. Maybe he borrowed it from one of the bag ladies under the viaduct. Madonna says Tango slept out a few nights down there with the bag ladies and the winos and the schizos because they had a bonfire and it was chilly in the Milkwhite Bread container. He may also have gone down for Sister's free soup, administered to the winos by the Geek. Sister's hot soup was an incentive for a lot of people.

Three o'clock, and Tango thought he was safe to be out and about from a Manus point of view and, given the area he was in, probably the cops as well (in so far as he ever felt safe from the cops) because the cops tend to stay off the Loop unless they are summoned, and then they come slowly, and in numbers, in the hope that whatever it is will have switched itself off before they get there. It saves time, paperwork and personal injuries to the force.

Tango turned off the Loop and he took the short cut over the waste ground. It was dark on the waste ground, the only light coming from the big fluorescent street lights running round the Loop, most of which weren't working.

Tango knew his way well, heading for the snapped off cherry tree.

Suddenly there was a terrible noise – a kind of honking.

"Jesus!" Tango thought. "What's that?"

The noise soared up the musical scale and switched from a honk to a scream to a screech that ended with a rattle, like some poor woman had just had a knife stuck in her throat.

Out of the dark, three figures loomed, walking straight at him, heading towards the Loop.

They were in no hurry. They came at him slowly, three of them, so he had nowhere to go.

Tango was stuck with his pram full of portaloo right in the path of these three figures, and they were converging on him, and he was seriously concerned for his liver and lights.

"*Knives*," Tango was thinking, scared out of his mind, so scared that he froze. His legs wouldn't go one way or the other, and they were nearly upon him.

All three bigger than him, approaching out of the dark, and behind them the sound still coming, a gasping, moaning sound.

Tango put his head down, so they'd see he couldn't see them, and maybe they would pass him by or maybe they wouldn't want to knife him.

"Evening," one of them said, though it was morning.

Tango knew the voice.

It was Alex Bakuli, dead Stevie's cousin.

Then they were past him, going slow.

He knew how lucky he was, and they knew, and they were letting him know they knew he knew, so he wouldn't get any funny ideas.

They went on over the waste ground.

Then they started to run.

Clatter, clatter, clatter of running feet down Stanley Street, away from the flats and the Loop.

Tango was shivering, blood-scared, his hands clamped on the handles of the pram. The moans were still going on.

"Don't want to be here!" was Tango's thought, but then there was the moaning and he thought he ought to look, though he didn't want to. Would someone come up when he was there and think it was him did it?

He didn't want to end up with a Bakuli beating either.

The moans got worse.

Someone was lying on the ground in a huddle by the bottom of number two stairs, Shaftesbury, well away from the fence.

The person had on a white coat but when Tango bent down to touch him the coat was all wet and that was because of the blood coming out of his arm, and the blood pouring down his face from his smashed nose and lips.

"Jumped off the landing, didn't I?" Manus told him. "Me bloody back's broke in two."

"I didn't even know it was Manus till he spoke," Tango says. "Couldn't see his face in the dark."

It wasn't just a beating that went wrong.

It was the result of Stevie Bakuli's name going in the Big Daddy Book.

CHAPTER
ELEVEN

"Why? Why? Why would anyone do that to my poor Manus?" moaned a distraught Mrs O in reception at the hospital. "The poor wee lamb."

She was in deep shock. With the massive weight of her and the way she was quivering and panting, Tango must have thought he'd wind up bringing her corpse home, as well as a mangled Manus.

"I'll never understand. I'll never understand," she wept at him.

Tango could have made a few suggestions, but he didn't. He just sat there clutching the poor lady's hand and trying to calm her down.

Meanwhile, up in theatre, they were stitching Manus' face back together as best they could considering the beating he had taken before he jumped off the landing at Shaftesbury. In his desperate efforts to escape from the Bakulis, he must have forgotten he was two floors up.

They could stitch his face, but there was nothing

much they could do for his back.

"What was he doing out there at that time in the morning?" Tango asked.

"I don't know," Mrs O said. "Who would do it? Why would they do it?"

All this, mind you, flowing over poor Tango, who not so long before had run off down the canal bank in his Y-fronts to get away from Manus.

The scene when Tango turned up on the O'Leary doorstep, having nipped out of the hospital before the cops came, must have been a good one.

Apparently Crystal was up feeding the baby and Mrs O was still in her pit, believing Manus to be in his.

Tango pounds on the door and Crystal opens it.

"Brian! What are you doing here? My mum will…"

Then she saw the blood down the front of his anorak.

"Oh, Brian!"

They were in the hallway and Tango was breaking the news to her when Mrs O came pounding down the stairs with her curlers in, intent on expelling Tango from the premises.

"Get outa my house! Get outa my house, you bastard!"

"Manus is hurt, Mum! Manus is hurt bad. Somebody beat him. He's in hospital."

"Manus is upstairs in his bed!"

But he wasn't.

"My Brian was really brilliant," Crystal told

Madonna. "He took Mum and he comforted her and told her Manus was going to be all right only he didn't let on how bad the back was. Then she wanted me to come to the hospital with her and I said I couldn't because of the baby and she said she wasn't going on her own and Brian said he couldn't go with her because of the cops and then she started crying and he said, well all right, he would go. I was really proud of Brian."

Tango, meet the cops!

Tango had reason to believe the cops might be after him, if they had word about Crystal being under-age, which he thought they might well have. Then there was the business about the beach hut break-ins as well, and the golf-club Bentley, and Tango being Tango there may have been a few other little matters outstanding, so the cops had him really worried. But it turns out they were nice as pie.

All sympathy, and could they give Mrs O a lift back home, because there was no point in hanging around when Manus was going to be heavily sedated for hours, and he ought to make sure she got some breakfast?

"I'm all right. I've had a cup of tea," from Mrs O.

"You need some food in you," from the cops, who were as concerned by her knocked-out appearance as Tango was.

"Take her home and get the doctor to her," they told Tango.

101

"I'm not going," stubbornly from Mrs O, bursting into floods of tears all over again.

"You're related?" the cops asked Tango.

"Well, sort of," Tango admitted, not wanting to commit himself on that ground.

"She needs to get her head down. Get her out of here. If she won't go home, take her across the road and get her a coffee and a bun. There's a cafe over there with soft seats – and keep her there till she's more herself."

"Yeah…" Tango said, doubtfully.

One of the cops, a young one, picked it up.

"No money, mate?"

Tango nodded.

So the cop gave him some.

It must have been the only time in his life Tango ever got something buckshee out of the cops, or anybody else in authority for that matter, barring Sam-Sam. The guy who gave it to him must have been a decent cop.

Tango and Mrs O ended up in the cafe across the road, with Tango trying to feed her some breakfast and Mrs O saying she felt sick and the man in the cafe anxious that she was going to throw up over his tables.

Mrs O was sitting there weeping when the decent cop came back. He started asking questions like who had it in for Manus?

There was no way Tango was even going to think the name Bakuli, let alone say it. The Bakulis have the Loop stitched up. Tango kept his mouth shut and Mrs O started weeping again. Then the cafe man got excited and wanted her out and the cop out and Tango out because they were upsetting people.

"No point in staying here, Missus," the decent cop told Mrs O, and he more or less manhandled her into his cop car.

So Tango got a free ride in a cop car back to Stanley Street where he ended up with Crystal and Mrs O and Baby D, trying to figure out what had happened.

The true story came right back to Crystal's clever idea, but Crystal never made the connection.

It turns out that among the letters of sympathy, Stevie Bakuli's mother had found one marked: RE: THE ESTATE OF STEPHEN RODERICK BAKULI, DECEASED. It asked what money there was and what provision had been made by his representatives for the upkeep and maintenance of Stephen Roderick Bakuli's child. The letter asked for a copy of Stevie's death certificate to prove that he was dead, and full details of any bequests or other claims against his estate the residue of which, in law, should be set aside for use of the said child, and would be taken account of in the granting of future public moneys to the mother of said child.

I haven't got that quite right because I didn't see the letter, but that was the gist of it – another pile driver in a plain envelope from the authorities who, as far as Mrs Bakuli was concerned, had hounded her son into the grave.

So the Bakulis made enquiries and there it was in black and white on the woman's desk:

Name and Occupation of Father: Stephen Roderick Bakuli – Deceased. Crystal's signature as Informant: C. O'Leary.

"Well, that is what the girl says, and she ought to know!" the woman behind the desk told Mrs Bakuli. "How can you be sure, anyway? Your son is dead, isn't he?"

I can't imagine any woman behind a desk being cruel enough to say that, but it is what she did say, according to Mrs Bakuli.

Mrs Bakuli went home to the family.

Reconstruction of what probably happened next:

"This little tramp O'Leary is trying to fix her kid on poor Stevie. Some little bitch from down Stanley Street he was at school with, and now she's trying to say he knocked her up."

"Related to big Manus, down the Builders' Arms? Those O'Learys?"

"Yeah. His sister! Manus probably poked his little sister himself!"

"This time Manus bloody O'Leary is going to get a lesson he won't forget. We've had bother with him in the past, but trying to land poor Stevie with his kid is right out of order!"

The considered opinion at the San Marino is that the Bakuli boys wouldn't have gone to all that trouble beating Manus just for the sake of Stevie's good name. There must have been more to it than that. But if there was, nobody knows what and Manus isn't saying, no doubt for his own good reasons.

"You must have seen these men. You must know who they were?" the cops said to Manus, when his mouth was fixed so he could slur out a few words.

"No. No way," from Manus, laying his head back on the pillow.

"You want somebody caught for this, don't you?"

Manus just shook his head.

"What are you mixed up in, O'Leary? You don't get a beating like that for nothing."

"Find out!" from Manus.

The cops drew their own conclusions but they never did find out for sure. They gave up on Manus.

The doctors let Manus out after a fortnight because they needed the bed, and all he could do for months was lie there, so they said he could do it at home, and they'd check him later and fix him up with some therapist, but it didn't seem to happen. Maybe the clerk lost the letter.

The odd pay-off of all this stuff is that Tango moved into the O'Leary's house, sharing with Crystal the best back room that used to belong to Manus. Manus was too far gone to whimper about it, let alone fist him out of it, and Mrs O had done a turn-around after Tango looked after her at the hospital.

She was frightened by what had happened to

Manus and she wanted a man about the place, so she thought she might as well accept the inevitable; Crystal had had a baby, Tango was the baby's father, and Tango was sticking by her daughter, so what else could she do?

For a brief period, Tango was the man of the house.

"Crystal asked me to come up and see Baby D, so I did," Madonna says. "Tango was down on the floor playing with little D, tickling his toes and making coo-coo noises. Mrs O all smiles, helping him with the nappies. Manus lying on his sofa looking like death warmed up, with Crystal feeding him soft prunes on a spoon because he couldn't feed himself and he was supposed to lie there for months without moving. It was like they had two babies in the house, not one."

Domestic bliss in Stanley Street.

A part of Mrs O was pleased as punch to have Manus safe at home under her eye all day, where he couldn't get a drink and therefore couldn't get himself into any more trouble.

It was "poor Manus" this, and "my poor Manus" that and "what will become of my poor crippled son?" all day, till Tango and Crystal were sick of it.

"God isn't finished with Manus yet, Mrs O'Leary," Sister Monica Rose told a tearful Mrs O, after Mrs O had been down to her flat and delivered several wet hankies full of her grief. "God loves us all."

"You're very good to me, Sister," quavered Mrs O.

"We'll do all we can to help you sort out your poor son's problems," from Sister Monica Rose.

Devotion to charity? Self appointed Sister Monica Rose of the Order of Saint Geek calling on all her innate goodness to do her selfless religious duty? Sister isn't ordinary organized religion; she and the Geek were a self-inspired and inspiring outfit all on their own, no call for the C. of E. or the Pope, but Madonna is certain-sure that Sister set out only with the idea of helping.

"I know she's trying to be a really good person," Madonna says. "She gets involved in other people's problems round the Loop flats because she believes in all that stuff."

"Oh, yeah?" Jackie Coney says. "I happen to know different! There'd been too many winos and schizos trotting up the stairs to the flat at Shaftesbury. Popeye and Olive Oyl had outstayed their welcome with the neighbours, and the authorities. Their time was up. The charity flat was being taken off them. So they had to relocate somewhere, hadn't they? That's what all that helping Manus stuff was about. Very practical lady, Olive Oyl is. She knows what side her bread is buttered."

But then, of course, Jackie Coney is a cynic, and a proven liar.

The next bit is the Gospel according to Crystal again, and it is interesting because of what she gives away about herself, as much as anything.

CHAPTER
TWELVE

Ten o'clock, and breakfast in bed for Crystal and Baby D, Tango having gone downstairs in his pyjama jacket and boxer shorts to fetch it, dropping in to check Manus in the front room and put him to rights while the kettle boiled. Tea and toast for Crystal and Manus, and a bottle for Baby D.

Tango is curled up with his toast on the end of the bed, holding Baby D, who is guzzling away at his bottle. Crystal is humped up clutching her knees, wondering what they can spare from the Giro for Baby D's first Christmas.

It *would* be Christmas. All good things come at Christmas.

Knock-knock on the door.

"Give me D!" Crystal said.

Tango kissed Baby D and handed him over.

"Cover yourself up!" Crystal giggled at him. "You don't know who might be at the door." She thought it might be Louise Brennan from the

Welfare again. There was a lot of hanky panky going on with Louise about getting them a place of their own and sorting out Tango's status so he could get a Giro now he had an address.

It was awkward, because Tango still thought the cops might be after him, but he didn't want to say so to Louise, who kept pushing forms at him to fill in. He got rid of the forms by posting them in his back pocket, but then she couldn't figure out why he got no response, and she was going to look into it for him. Mrs O wasn't supposed to know it was going on, because what they were after was alternative accommodation. Basically Crystal and Tango were both fed up with lifting and laying Manus, which Tango had to do mostly. That was partly because he was used to that sort of work with his grannie, and partly because the other two couldn't lift Manus. Manus was a dead weight who had to be handled carefully and Tango was always good at being gentle. He could have made a male nurse, if only Sam-Sam had been able to get him pointed in that direction, which he hadn't.

Knock-knock again, insistently. They had a bell but it didn't work, because of damp in the wiring.

Manus added to the chorus with his sofa-side bell ding-donging urgently, to try to attract their attention. Manus was a great man with the bell. His hand was never off it, wanting something, ding-donging to establish that his needs were paramount and he was still alive.

"Hurry up, Brian!" from Crystal, as he reached

for his jeans. "The noise'll wake Mum."

Mrs O was always a late sleeper. There wasn't a lot to get up for.

Tango abandoned the jeans and draped Crystal's dressing-gown round him. The dressing-gown was his present for Crystal when she was in hospital. He was always giving her little things to make her feel good when she was down, which was often enough. Better not ask where the money came from. Nobody knows, probably Hank was behind it. Which begs the question: what was Tango's business relationship with Hank anyway? There's a limit to what you can earn round a used car lot. That must remain one of the great Tango mysteries.

"You look gorgeous, Brian!" Crystal mocked him. "Louise will get a thrill!"

Coming out of the bedroom, Tango heard a key in the lock and the street door opening. That stopped him. Then there was the sound of the front room door and somebody greeting Manus, so it wasn't a break-in … but who had got hold of a key?

Tango bumped down the stairs, all big knees and bare feet, feeling foolish in Crystal's flouncy dressing-gown.

There was mumbling coming from the front room.

Tango barged in.

Sister Monica Rose was sitting on the floor beside Manus' sofa. Manus lived and slept on a board on the sofa because Tango couldn't safely move him upstairs. He was on the sofa because the frame-bed Louise Brennan was trying to get them hadn't come yet and would be another three weeks at least. That meant the family were short of a sofa, and there were only the two soft chairs. Tango had got a wonky car seat from Hank's pile and they had put that on the floor, so it hid the baby's nappy bucket, and that meant the whole family could sit in comfort and watch *Strike it Lucky* on TV.

Sister was holding Manus' hand. She'd placed a rectangular silver plaque on the TV tray that rested on Manus' lap. It had a little bell fixed on top, and the sign of the fish engraved on the silver.

The Geek was kneeling on the floor in front of Manus, reciting something.

He didn't stop when Tango came in. Sister put her finger to her lips and smiled a tight little icy smile at Tango. Then she took in the sight of his bare knees beneath the dressing-gown frills, and she frowned. She motioned at him with her hands and eyes, a downward movement.

He reckoned she was telling him to sit down, so he sat in Mrs O's chair; then he saw she was still signalling him down off the chair, motioning him forward.

"I got down on the floor, didn't I?" he told Crystal later. "I couldn't figure it. It was like some kind of prayer meeting. I'd been staying clear of Mrs O's stuff with Sister, but this time I reckoned I was caught."

Mumbo-mumbo-mumbo from the Geek, bending tight in close to Manus' head, and passing his hands up and down the length of Manus' body.

"Kind of stroking the air above him," Tango says. Then:

"Amen," said the Geek.

"Amen," said Sister.

"Amonn," mumbled Manus, who had a tooth or two missing, and had the stitches on his face to consider, so his speech was still difficult, although that side effect of the beating was beginning to wear off.

"So I said 'Amen' too," Tango told Crystal. "I didn't know what they were at; it wasn't the same as at funerals and things, but I thought I'd better say it so they wouldn't be upset, seeing they were funny in the head."

The Geek got up from the floor, nodded at Tango, and sat down in the other armchair, putting his head back and closing his eyes.

Sister got up, as Tango was ungracefully unwinding himself, trying to preserve decency for her sake by keeping his knees together, while clutching the divide in Crystal's dressing-gown.

Jackie Coney had the name about right, he was thinking. Olive Oyl was it. Sister was thin as a stick, very neatly dressed in her neat, dark mackintosh, with lapels open at the top to show a white roll-neck sweater. She didn't wear a cross. She had a miniature of the silver thing she'd put on the table dangling from a plain chain round her neck.

"Is there somewhere we could talk privately,

Mr Tangello?" she said. "I mean *now*, while we have the opportunity?"

In charge, you see. That was the thing that struck Tango. Also he didn't know what opportunity she was on about.

"She just took everything over," Crystal told Madonna. "It was wild. She rail-roaded Tango in the kitchen and gave him a long speech about how she'd been doing her best to help my mum and Manus and there were things she had to say to him, if he couldn't see them for himself. Then she started giving off about the state things were in with the nappy bucket stinking and the curtains still over at ten o'clock so light couldn't get in."

"Hold on, Missus," Tango said. "I'm only up out of bed."

"I can see that, Mr Tangello," she said. "I've only got to look at the state of this kitchen!"

The house was never too tidy in the time Tango was there, Madonna says, and what with the baby things and Manus as a full time invalid and keeping the windows closed, maybe it was a bit niffy, but then it was a quarter past ten in the morning and Mrs O hadn't got up yet so things hadn't been put to rights.

"Listen, Missus," Tango said. "I haven't got you figured. Like we'd have had the place tidy, but you wasn't expected. Crystal would have had things put to rights, but she had a bad night with the baby, so I told her to stay in bed."

It is interesting but hardly a startling revelation

that Tango saw complaints about the state of the house as an attack on Crystal, not himself. Knowing Tango, I'd say he did the housework not-too-badly when he got round to it, but it was something he did *for* Crystal, because she was worn out with the baby, not because it was there to be done.

"Manus must be *properly* cared for, Mr. Tangello," Sister said. "I don't think you or Crystal are doing as much as you might to help poor Mrs O'Leary."

"You know nothing about us!" Tango told her, angrily.

"Oh, I know all about *you*, Mr. Tangello," she said.

Tango knew this was meant to be a big downer, but of course he didn't know what the "all" meant, so she had him badly on the back foot. There are "alls" and "alls", and the "all" she knew could have included things he didn't want anyone to hear about, particularly Crystal.

"It's not my house," Tango said, not quite sure what he was supposed to be defending, or why. Up to now if he'd thought about Sister at all it was as the woman who looked after the down and outs and helped people with the Welfare. Now, in her prim way, she seemed to be turning nasty.

"Indeed not, Mr Tangello," she said. "So far as I am concerned you are a not very welcome guest in Mrs O'Leary's home. Have you yet obtained employment, Mr Tangello?"

"What is this?" from Tango.

"You have fathered a child, Mr Tangello," she said. "God has given you that gift. May he give you the grace to pull yourself together and make something of your life, and that of the unfortunate young woman who is *your* responsibility."

"Eh?" from Tango.

Then she seemed to go crazy. She started spouting words he couldn't understand. She was rattling the words out and he thought it was some kind of curse, and she was waving her hands about in front of him, making passes in the air, and clutching at the silver symbol on the chain round her neck.

She was wagging it at him, when Crystal marched in with Baby D in her arms. She'd been out on the stairs listening and she'd had enough.

"Hold him!" Crystal told Tango, and she pushed Baby D into his arms, and took command of the situation.

"You, out!" she bawled at Sister Monica Rose, bundling her out of the kitchen.

Shouting, banging of doors, the Geek and Sister forcibly expelled into the street, with Manus from his set position on the sofa impotently asking to be told what was happening, but to no avail.

Crystal came storming back in, flushed with success.

Tango was standing there, bare-kneed in her frilly dressing-gown, jogging the child absent-mindedly and wondering what the hell was going on.

"Give me the baby," she ordered Tango. Then she gave him a mouthful. "What do you think you're doing, standing there and letting that woman say things like that about me in my own home?" Crystal blazed at him. I can just see Tango standing there, with all that bursting over his head, wondering what had happened to the little lost girl weeping for her daddy he had comforted on their love seat down by the canal bank.

Tango knew he was in trouble, but he didn't know what for.

"Magdalene!" Crystal said. "She called me a Magdalene."

Tango hadn't heard. It had been said as Crystal bundled them out.

"But your name's not Magdalene," Tango said, totally confused.

"Oh shit, Tango!" Crystal said. "What way were you brought up? Were you never in a church at all?"

Which was about right. He never had been. Crystal knew that well enough. It was one of Mrs O's spiritual points when she was in her anti-Tango spell. Tango wasn't even a collapsed Christian like his Auntie Flo; he was no-God-and-never-had-one like most people on the Loop.

Crystal, of course, was a nominal Catholic, though she'd not been to Mass since her daddy took her one Christmas night as a treat. He held her up at the back of the crowd so she could see the Mysteries, and he swayed because of the amount of

116

drink he had on him. The swaying scared the wits out of the five-year-old Crystal, and she started crying, but he wouldn't put her down till the Mass was finished. Everybody was glaring at him and Crystal never forgot it. She forgave her Daddy because he was the one who loved her but it put her off going to church, though Mrs O had fed her a lot of the half-remembered bits, including, apparently, who the Magdalene was.

"A Magdalene is a penny-in-the-slot merchant like Funny Bum!" Crystal said furiously. "On the game! Open your legs for anyone. That's what she was calling me, and you are standing there listening to it and saying 'Oh, yes?' and you're the one what done it to me and you're the one who is supposed to stand up for me."

And she was crying in his arms, with the baby cradled in between them, both their bodies on it, warm together, with the words of the woman locked away, outside their little Trinity.

The revealing thing to my mind is Crystal's own telling of the story. She is there giving the orders, and Tango is lost and confused in the middle of it all. She gives him the baby, she fights, she snatches it back from him, she tongue lashes him, and then she's back being comforted by him again, as if she'd run out of emotional puff. Crystal was changing all right. She hadn't come to the end of loving Tango, she still needed him, but she was on her way there, nonetheless, and beginning to figure out who the strong party was in their relationship.

That seemed at the time to be the sum of Sister Monica Rose's visit.

"We never thought she'd dare show her face again in Stanley Street after the mouthful I gave her," Crystal told Madonna, ruefully.

What they hadn't reckoned on was Mrs O.

Showdown in the kitchen, two days later, 23rd December:

"Manus needs Sister," from Mrs O, responding to Crystal's demand that Sister should hand back the front door key which Mrs O had given her.

"What bloody for, Mummy?" brutally from Crystal, who had just been informed that Sister Monica Rose was to be given the run of the house any time she came calling.

"Well, she helps him with his problem," awkwardly, from Mrs O.

"He has enough of them!" Crystal snapped. "Always had."

"His special problem," Mrs O said.

"*Which* one?"

"Like your daddy," Mrs O said. "Only Manus knows Sister was helping him get better."

"Better of *what*?" Crystal said. "Drink again?"

"He was afraid he'd hurt somebody," Mrs O said. "When he had a drink in him. So he swore to me he wasn't going back on the bottle after the night he chased Brian. Sister's helping him come off it."

"*Back* on the bottle?" Crystal said scornfully. "He was never off it."

"He was sober the night he was beat," Mrs O insisted.

The bottom line was this:

"Manus needs Sister," from Mrs O. "It's my house and Manus is my son!"

"I'm your daughter," Crystal pointed out, wagging the baby at her. "I'm your daughter, and this one here is your grandson. Do we count for nothing?"

"It's my house," from Mrs O. "You'll do what I say in my house, and you'll let in who I want."

"She's not coming here and saying I'm on the game."

"How do I know you're not?" devastatingly from Mrs O. "Your friend *Miss* Johnston is, so maybe you are at it too!"

Yelling and screaming from Crystal.

The almost incredible outcome was Crystal snatching up the baby and walking out, throwing her door key at her mother.

"Oh, you'll be back!" from Mrs O, disdainfully.

"I'll never be back! Never ever!" from Crystal. "I wouldn't stay one night more in this house nursing bloody Manus if you paid me. You can nurse him yourself if you love him so much, and I hope he dies of the drink, just like my daddy!"

She wouldn't go back.

Maybe she wanted to, when she'd cooled down, Madonna says, but her pride wouldn't let her.

She left the baby with Madonna and Myrtle in Myrtle's house and she went off to cut short

Hank's pre-Christmas party in his hut and tell Tango they hadn't a roof over their heads any more.

Crystal made Tango go and pick up her stuff and the baby's things and Mrs O never said a word to him. She let him in, frozen faced, and she stood and watched him, but she never twitched a lip except to say:

"You're the one that's ruined my boy's life, you bastard!" as he was going out the door.

And, yes, it *was* just coming up to Christmas, it *would* be, and it was bitter cold. Funny Bum had her kids out on Christmas day-loan from the welfare and with Tango's grannie already at the flat her place was bunged out. Tango knew he couldn't ask her anyway. The Welfare were keeping close tabs and already sniffing at Grannie T and her portaloo. There was no way Myrtle's mum would have had them. Madonna had no way of helping, given the overcrowding that already existed in the flat in Nightingale.

No room at the inn for Tango's family.

"Well, we could sleep in the old Milkwhite Bread container down the back of the yard," Tango told her.

Hank wasn't having that. Hank again. He had no kids, Hank. Maybe that had something to do with it. He got a kick out of kind of adopting Tango, and helping with the big guy's problems.

"Do you really believe that, Chris?" Madonna said to me once. "From where you sit Tango can

120

do no wrong, can he? I think Tango played on old Hank's generosity for all he was worth, at every opportunity."

"That's not the Tango I know!" I objected.

"It's the Tango Crystal talks about now!" she said.

"If they exploited Hank, then Crystal put Tango up to it," I said. "She was the manipulator. Tango wouldn't know how to start! He was never in Crystal's league once she found herself and got going."

"You really don't like Crystal, do you?" she said.

"I don't like the way she treated Tango," I said.

Whatever about that, and whoever put the squeeze on Hank, it worked. He insisted that they take over his office hut, because he wouldn't be open Christmas Eve or Christmas Day. It meant that they had to be out the second day after Boxing Day.

The baby got a lot of little plastic toys and a teddy bear from Tango and Crystal, but there was no present from his Grannie O'Leary. Baby D's Christmas present remained gaily wrapped in Christmas paper on the table in the kitchen at Mrs O's house.

Mrs O was in no mood to deliver it, being made of the same stern stuff as her erring daughter. To my mind, they deserved each other.

It wasn't a very merry Christmas, but it wasn't a totally black time for Tango and Crystal either.

They stayed huddled in Hank's office with their wonderful Baby D to warm them, and they had each other without anyone else to come between them, but the big, big, big plus was the unexpected party in the San Marino, one of the happy interludes in their story.

Despite all the sink-estate stuff that went on in the papers, people are warm and kind to each other and show compassion most of the time, even in a place like Buffey's Loop. The most unexpected people doing their damnedest to make awful situations like Tango's better: that is the cement that holds the Loop world together, when by rights it ought to split apart.

In this case the guy with the big heart was Jackie Coney, who wasn't supposed to have one.

CHAPTER
THIRTEEN

If the San Marino dinner party sounds wildly unlikely, it is nonetheless what happened, and Jackie made it happen.

A lonely Jackie Coney, chucked out of the Coney household after the usual Boxing Day morning scenery with his dad, had made his way round the dead Estate looking for company. He took a festive notion and armed himself with some cans for Tango and Crystal and a plastic Christmas tree for Baby D.

Jackie visited them in Hank's hut.

Boxing Day cheer was thin in the hut. Cold turkey had been donated by Funny Bum, after Tango and Crystal and Baby D had been round to her flat for Christmas dinner. Tango had been sent out hunting the streets for a machine that worked now that Crystal was hooked on fags. Crystal crouched in the office swivel chair, shivering over Hank's little one bar electric fire, and the baby had an incipient sniffle.

"They'd no TV, no nothing!" Jackie reported. Clearly absence of a TV impressed him most of all, Boxing Day being cartoon time.

What Jackie did next was get up and go, when nobody else was doing a thing for them, bar Hank.

"It's real bad in there," Jackie told Melons. "Like grim bad. We're supposed to be his mates and we're going to do something about it so they have a proper Christmas lash!"

"Christmas is over," Melons pointed out.

"Principle's the same," Jackie said. "We'll get all Tango's and Crystal's mates and have a real go and everyone will get boozed!"

The Builders' Arms wouldn't wear it because they didn't do catering and there was no way the party would fit into Funny Bum's with the portaloo, so Jackie went in and bullied Bernarde at the San Marino to lay on the works, egg mayonnaise and all.

"We want it special for Tango and Crystal so they'll remember the baby's first Christmas," Jackie told Bernarde.

"Who's paying?" Bernarde said.

"Everybody is paying their own whack except Tango and Crystal and Tango's old grannie," Jackie said. "Paper hats and all. Table for nine."

The nine were to be Tango and Crystal and Funny Bum, Melons, Jackie, Madonna and Myrtle, the Major and Grannie T.

"And Baby D makes ten, but you'll never charge for a baby!" Jackie told Bernarde.

Bernarde made a face.

"Screw you, Bernarde," Jackie said cheerfully. "And we want Christmas discount too, because you'll be rid of all your left-over turkey and stuffing."

"Bernarde did a real good job," Madonna says. "No soggy peas or turnip. Turkey, sprouts, carrots in butter, stuffing, Christmas pud, all the trimmings. He even threw in some crackers. Only the plonk was funny. Jackie swore it was kosher, but it did my head in next day. Jackie picked it up cheap somewhere and we had it on the table in big plastic Coke bottles in case any nosy bugger walked in." That was to get round the problem of the drink licence, which Bernarde hadn't got, another negotiating battle which Jackie won.

The remaining problem was Grannie T.

"She's too frail to be taken out," Funny Bum told Jackie Coney.

"There's no way we're having the party without her!" Jackie said. "You know what Tango's like."

So Jackie got Funny Bum to work her wiles on the Major. Jackie and Melons carried Grannie T down the stairs from Funny Bum's flat and they drove her in the Major's car straight to the front door of the San Marino. Funny Bum had her all cleaned and polished for the occasion, wearing the brooch Tango had bought her for Christmas as a badge of love. Jackie stuck a paper hat on her head and handed her one of Bernarde's crackers and a coke-glass full of wine, so that she was all geared up like the Spirit of Christmas when Tango and Crystal arrived.

Nobody told Crystal and Tango till the last minute. The Major and Funny Bum whisked them away from the tin of Christmas macaroni they were heating up on the ring in Hank's office.

"It sounds stupid, but it was really nice," Melons says. "We got slewed on the stuff in Bernarde's coke bottles and we were singing Christmas carols. The only worry was whether Grannie T would tip off her chair and fall dead on us. Funny Bum was having fits and telling her to go easy, and Grannie T was grinning and tossing it back. Baby D was passed round like a parcel till Tango stopped it. He sat with the baby on his knee and he had his arm round his old grannie. He was whispering to her and hugging her and blowing her kisses from the baby, and the big guy looked really happy – so did the old lady for that matter. As far as she was concerned the sun shone out of Tango's backside."

After the party the Major took the totally plastered Grannie T and Funny Bum home and then he came back to the cafe for Crystal and Tango and Baby D.

The excitement and the glow of the party was melting off Crystal, like snow in the gutter. They'd been chucked out of Mrs O's house on the 23rd, when the Welfare was all closed up, and she was planning to be there first thing the next morning when they opened again, but meanwhile there was nothing they could do and their domestic circumstances were getting to Crystal.

"It's a muck heap of a place," Crystal told Tango.

"Hank's been real good letting us have it," Tango said.

"Yeah, *but...*" Crystal said.

Tango put his arm round Crystal and hugged her, but he knew that there wasn't much else he could do, barring a fairy godmother, which he hadn't got – or at least, he believed he hadn't got one, which isn't quite the same thing. Fairy godmothers come in all sorts of unexpected packs, and this one ran on batteries.

The Major phut-phut-phutted his little Orion down the Dock Road as if he was going to pull to a stop in front of Hank's big sign, but then he went on past it, with an ecstatic grin on his face and his teeth a-wobble, which was always a sign of growing excitement with the Major.

"Hey, Major! Stop!" Tango said.

"We're here, Major," from a down-in-the-mouth Crystal.

"Not tonight, my dear!" said the Major.

The next thing they knew they had pulled up outside the Major's house in Somerset Gardens. The Major led them in through the hall and down to his back room and there was everything the way Funny Bum and the Major had worked it out. A big double bed and two soft chairs, a cupboard and a table and a Dimplex so Baby D would be warm. The Christmas tree from Funny Bum's flat had done a flit now her kids had gone back, and stood framed in the window, so that the fairy lights glittered out onto the patch of garden.

There was even an ash tray for Crystal's fags.

"Your new home, till you get fixed up!" the Major said. "You can put the baby out to air in the back!"

Tango and Crystal didn't know what to do with themselves.

Crystal started crying all over the Major, and Tango stood there clutching Baby D with his big mouth open, trying to say something but not bringing it off. The blood had flooded up into his cheeks and his eyes glistened through his sello-taped glasses.

Old Mrs the Major put her head round the door, balancing her sparrow thin body on her stick because of the arthritis.

"Is this our happy family, Cecil?" she said to the Major.

The only sad bit about this is Funny Bum having to be kept away, so Mrs the Major wouldn't know about her part in it.

"I think Mrs the Major knew about Funny Bum all along," Madonna says. "Mrs the Major was a lot brighter than the Major. I don't think she minded sharing him if it let her off having to go and sit in the Builders' Arms. She was happy as long as the Major was happy."

It is still a shame about Funny Bum though – she should have been there to see the look on Crystal's face.

CHAPTER
FOURTEEN

"Of course, it boomeranged!" Madonna says. "Crystal and Tango got put down the bottom of the housing list because the Welfare had people sleeping out, and Crystal and Tango had a roof over their heads."

"Well, we'll move out and sleep in a box then!" Crystal told Louise Brennan. "Then you'll have to house us. We can't go on living with the Major. It isn't fair. They only have the three rooms, and three of us in one of them."

Louise had to tell them that wouldn't work; the Big Boots' Rule Book would count them as voluntarily homeless if they moved out of the Major's flat, and that meant their entitlement to housing was down the chute.

"You're no help at all!" Crystal told her. "We ought to dump on your doorstep!"

Crystal did her tears bit. That turned on Tango's big-man-protecting-Crystal act and he gave Louise the back end of his tongue. She had him chucked out.

"Things always get worse in these cases," Louise told Madonna. "It just goes wrong. The next thing was that I put the forms through about their change of address, but the forms got stuck in the machine somewhere, and Crystal's next Giro went to her mother's house."

This was just after their bust-up with Louise, and Tango being warned off the premises, so they were afraid to go back to the office. They were both scared of Louise anyway, because she talked in sentences and made them sign forms, and every time they signed one it felt like giving a bit of themselves away.

So the Giro was in Mrs O's house. At least that's what they were told when Crystal telephoned the Welfare.

"I'm not going back to that house!" Crystal told Madonna, in a panic.

"Well, *somebody* will have to go and fetch it!" Madonna said.

"I know that," Crystal said.

"Where's Brian?" Madonna said, because she absolutely didn't want the job. She was getting a bit fed up with being constantly involved in the Tango/Crystal saga.

"It's no good asking Brian anything about money," Crystal said. "He doesn't really understand that stuff, buying baby things and all. It costs, you know."

"Seems to be able to lay hands on it when he needs it," Madonna said, a little sourly. Madonna had money problems of her own. She had taken a weekend job to help out at home, and she says she was irritated by the way Tango and Crystal seemed to think money would drop on their heads if they just told people they needed some.

"Brian can't go on borrowing from Hank. We've had too much off him already. We need money of our own, and we won't have any till we get my Giro coming regularly. I've got to have my Giro," Crystal said. The clear implication was that she, Madonna, should do something about it, and Madonna was determined not to let herself get sucked in.

"What about his?" Madonna countered.

"His what?"

"Brian's. Brian's Giro."

Awkward silence.

"He doesn't get one," Crystal said.

"Why not?" said Madonna. "He must be entitled to something, surely?"

Crystal hesitated before replying, as if she was afraid of letting the conversation drift into a jar-of-worms mode.

"I told him," Crystal said, after a long pause. "Only he's not entitled, he says. And he won't go near the Welfare again."

"What? Why?"

"*Because...*" Crystal said, very down in the mouth.

"Because *what*?" Madonna said, really puzzled. Tango had no money, and no job, and no visible means of support, so of course he was entitled, the way Madonna saw it. "What's he done?"

"I don't know what he's done," Crystal said, looking down at her feet. She started inspecting the sole of her shoe, and picking at it with one long nail.

"Well, you ask him," Madonna said, impatiently. "I mean he must know. If he did something and the Welfare are after him, he must know what he's done."

"The cops were at his auntie's house," Crystal said. Note it was "the cops" not "the Welfare", so the ground had unsubtly switched, and Madonna recognized it.

"Brian must know what about," Madonna said, with a sinking feeling.

There was a long silence.

"He done the bike shop," Crystal said eventually. "Down the High Street. And he thinks they're on to him."

"Oh bugger," Madonna said. "What did he nick?"

Crystal face's cleared. "He didn't *steal* anything, like pinch stuff. Brian wouldn't do that. He thinks too much of me and Baby D to do that. He put a brick through the window. Chucked this brick. Because of the Bakulis."

"Eh?"

"He said it was Stevie's family who done our

133

Manus. Brian said we owed them one. So he took this brick and he chucked it through the bike shop window so they'd know the O'Leary's aren't soft touches. Only he got it wrong."

"How come?"

"Wrong bloody bike shop," Crystal said. "Just like Brian! The Bakulis don't own it any more. Not since long before Stevie died. You know my Brian," she added, hopelessly. "How do I know what he's been doing?"

"Well, you go down the Welfare and you tell them your mum has stolen your Giro and they'll put a stop on it and they'll give you another one."

"They won't do nothing," Crystal said.

Then Tango came waltzing in, doing his funny Tango-walk, and waiting for applause, which he didn't get.

"What's up, Doc?" he asked brightly.

"You've got to go and get my Giro from Mum, Brian, pronto!" Crystal said. "That's what's up! You've got to go. I'm not arguing about it, Brian. I'm *telling* you, so there!"

"Yeah. Well, I will, won't I?" Tango said. "Sure I will. It's our money. I'm not scared of your mum!"

Then he went into his big-guy act again, for Madonna's benefit, not Crystal's. I think even Tango knew Crystal had long ago seen through it.

"I'll sort it out, I will," he said. "The whole lot. Your mum and the Welfare, everybody. They're not messing me around no more."

"Yes, well, you do that, Brian," Madonna said. "Take it all in hand."

She says Tango missed the acid in that one.

"Somebody's got to do it," Tango swaggered. "It's not right. Me and Crystal need that money and I'm going to tell them. I will. I'll show them they can't muck us about no more. Yeah! Yeah! I know my rights. I need that money for Crystal and my baby!"

"God, I could kill Brian when he comes on like that!" Crystal said glumly, when he'd gone.

"It's OK, so long as he gets your Giro," Madonna said.

"Yeah. I suppose so," Crystal said, and she started feeding the baby.

Apparently Tango got short shrift at Mrs O's house. Sister Monica Rose wouldn't open the door to him.

"It's Crystal's money!" Tango yelled through the letterbox at her.

"It's owed for the back rent for your room," Sister Monica Rose yelled back.

Then Tango banged on the door and called her a few names, and the door opened. If Tango thought he could barge past Sister Monica Rose and grab Crystal's Giro he had another think coming, because it was the Geek who confronted him.

The big Geek told Tango he would hammer him if Tango didn't clear off. So much for gentle Jesus.

Tango cleared off without Crystal's Giro, bugging off in the face of any adversity, in this instance heading for his other house, where his grannie would hold his hand and tell him he was her good boy.

Funny Bum and the Major were there. The story came out of Tango in jerks but when Funny Bum got the gist of it she frowned, because she could see Tango was sitting there in little pieces, not knowing what to do. She sensed he was close to tears, and of course the old lady was working herself into a state in sympathy.

"Don't you cry, Gran. Don't you cry, or you'll have me crying too," Tango told her gently.

Funny Bum couldn't take it. There was no point in her waiting for Tango to grow up, and she didn't want Grannie T to have any more upset.

It was all landed on Funny Bum's mat, yet again.

"What could I do?" she says, echoing Madonna. "Brian had obviously run out of ideas. I reckoned Crystal had been slagging him, and that was what was behind it. The one thing he could never take was when she told him home truths. He had to have her buttering him up, and she hadn't time for that any more. She had too much to worry about. I was hoping he'd get the message and sort things out himself, but what was the point of hoping, when he wasn't making any moves?"

In other words, Crystal had undermined poor Tango. Funny Bum and Madonna had both seen it happen, and they should have tipped Crystal off. If she'd backed the big guy instead of getting at him, things might have been different.

"Yes, Chris, and pigs might fly!" Madonna says. "He had to start trying to stand on his own feet. They are big enough."

"That's just what he was doing," I said. "Crystal should have backed him. He'd have found a way out. She was on an ego-trip, at his expense, taking over his big man bit, so she would look clever. She knew all his faults when she started out…"

"That was before the baby," Madonna said.

"What difference does that make?"

"She had the bloody baby, Chris! Life stopped being a big game for Crystal, after the baby. It wakened her up. He was full of talk, but she was the one who had borne the child, and when it came out of her body she was the one who had to buy it stuff and start thinking about their future."

"The big guy wanted to do that. He would have, if she'd let him. It might have been his usual muddle, but that would have been better for all of them than…"

"Brian was all talk, no do!" Madonna told me sharply, and she wouldn't be budged from her opinion.

Anyway, Funny Bum found herself coping with the mess Crystal's ego act had made of poor Tango. I know for a fact that Funny Bum puts a lot of it down to Crystal, but there she was with Brian and Grannie T sitting there comforting each other, and meanwhile no Giro.

Funny Bum gave in.

"Me and the Major will get Crystal's Giro, Tango. Won't we, Major?" she said firmly, although the Major didn't look too certain.

"There, now, Brian!" said the old lady, suddenly all smiles.

"You can stay here and keep me company while Iris is gone."

So Grannie T was well pleased anyway, sitting beaming at the thought of another half hour with her favourite boy.

"Yeah, but..." Tango objected half-heartedly.

"Never you worry yourself, Brian dear," said Funny Bum, patting his head, but not without a little note of sarcasm in her voice. "Just you keep a hold of your old gran's hand, eh? Keep her happy till I come back." She'd been rail-roaded into it and she wanted Tango to know she wasn't pleased, but she didn't think it had sunk in, somehow.

"You bring it back here to me, so I can give it to Crystal," Tango said, brightening up.

Funny Bum dressed the Major up in his coat and hat and off they went, leaving Tango to put the plastic bib on his gran so he could feed her her Complan with her teddy-bear spoon.

He felt safe, doing that. The other, the Giro and the Geek and Crystal's mum, was something he couldn't cope with.

No answer when Funny Bum and the Major knock-knocked at Mrs O's door.

No lights on.

"They *need* that money, Major," from Funny

Bum. "Poor little thing, Crystal, with the baby and all. And Mrs O has no right to it. It doesn't belong to her. It is Crystal's Giro, for the baby. And we're going to get it!"

She led the Major down the alley at the back of Stanley Street.

The yard door was open, Funny Bum says, so they didn't have to climb on bins or anything like that.

"Take care, my dear," from the Major, hanging back as Funny Bum tried the back door, which leads into the little kitchen.

"It won't budge, Major," Funny Bum said. "Can't *you* do something?" Funny Bum was posing as the maiden in distress, which is her usual way of stirring the Major.

The Major tried rattling the door, but it wouldn't open.

"Break it down?" Funny Bum suggested.

The poor Major bumped his shoulder against the door, very carefully, and then said it wouldn't break, sounding apologetic.

"What about the window up there?" Funny Bum said, pointing up at the bathroom window.

"Well, *if* we had a ladder, the Major said, doubtfully. This is all as related by Funny Bum to Madonna. Madonna says she figures the Major was trying to show willing, but not actually break into the house, because being a burglar isn't the Major's style, but if he was doing that, Funny Bum trumped him.

"Hold on a minute, Major," Funny Bum said, and she went into the back alley.

She came back clutching a ladder.

Gingerly, the Major ascended it.

He eased the window open, got into Mrs O's bathroom, out onto the landing, down the stairs, and opened the back door for Funny Bum. No wonder it wouldn't budge. It had three big security bolts, which must have been fitted by the Geek.

"Now, where is it, Major dear?" Funny Bum said, looking round her. They had the door wide open so they could scarper, though Funny Bum had her doubts about the Major's scarperability.

"I feel a bit wheezy, my dear," the Major said, and he sat down on a chair. It wasn't every day the Major climbed up a ladder and broke into someone's house, and he was eighty-something.

"I knew I had to be quick," Funny Bum told Madonna.

Funny Bum started looking for the Giro, but she was afraid to put the kitchen light on, in case she would be spotted.

No Giro in the kitchen.

Out into the hall.

No Giro.

Into the front room.

"Keep away! Keep away from me!" from the figure lying on the sofa in the dark.

"Bloody Manus," Funny Bum told Madonna. "I *knew* he had the front room, I just forgot. Then I was in there, and he was scared sick because he thought I was the Bakulis or somebody come to do him again. He was more scared than I was."

"It's all right," from Funny Bum.

"Keep away from me!" almost crying, from Manus on the the sofa.

"He couldn't move because of his back, poor bugger," Funny Bum told Madonna. "He's lying there with someone creeping into his room. He must have thought I was going to batter him over the head and kill him."

"Sorry, Manus," Funny Bum said, and she tip-toed out of the room.

Manus started shouting.

"Come on Major, it's no go!" Funny Bum told him, and they were out the back door and down the yard, leaving the ladder propped against the window.

"Really daft, it was!" Funny Bum says. "But I didn't think there was any harm done. It was dark in the front room, there was no way Manus would know it was me, unless he had recognized my voice, and I didn't think he would."

So how come when Mrs O and Sister Monica Rose came home they found that Manus had rolled himself off the sofa, and was cowering behind it in the dark, whimpering with fear, his story being that Tango and Crystal had broken into Crystal's own house, and that *Tango* spoke to him, and he thought Tango had come threatening to finish him off?

"'Sorry Manus' is all I said!'" Funny Bum

141

insists. "The Major never came in the room, or spoke at all. How could Manus mistake me for Tango?"

It seems incredible to me, but Manus' version is the officially accepted one, as disseminated by Sister Monica Rose, who promptly took charge of the situation and went down the road to telephone for the police.

It was Funny Bum's burglary that really broke things up for Tango and Crystal. It was the beginning of the end.

CHAPTER FIFTEEN

What happened next is full of confusion, because the main word we have on it comes from Crystal, in two separate versions: one as conveyed to Madonna, whom she regarded as her respectable friend; and the other to Funny Bum, who knew the score where Tango was concerned.

"D wouldn't sleep," Crystal told Madonna. "I didn't want to wake Mrs the Major again, because she'd already had two nights up with us, so I thought I would take the baby out and just wheel him round the streets, and I did."

That's the public version, accounting for Crystal and Baby D being out at six o'clock on a January morning.

"Me and Brian had words," a weepy Crystal told Funny Bum later on. "Hank had been round. There was some stuff missing, and he wanted to talk to Brian about it."

"What kind of stuff?" Funny Bum asked her,

because she too had heard all kinds of speeches from Tango and Crystal about Tango being a reformed character because of being D's Daddy.

"It was the petty cash, from Hank's drawer," Crystal told her. "Just a few quid, but it was the principle of the thing. Hank had been helping us and all."

Tango told her he'd taken the money all right, but he said it was money Hank owed him and it was the usual arrangement that he could take small sums from the petty cash and leave a note saying what he'd taken and fix it with Hank later.

"Well, that isn't what Hank's saying," Crystal told him.

"He owed it me!" Tango said, really losing his rag. Then he added, "Anyway, I'd have put it back when we got your Giro."

"You stole money from Hank."

"I never."

"Well, it's gone, and where is it?"

"Hank'll get it back. It's only a loan. Hank shouldn't have been on at you about it. Hank knows the score."

"You know what it was, don't you Chris?" Madonna said to me, a long time later. "That's the money he gave Myrtle. The instalment on GS241."

Crystal had been looking at Myrtle's mum's catalogue with Tango. There was a sapphire ring in it, and Crystal made eyes at it. GS241 was the catalogue number.

144

"That's beautiful," she said. "I'd love a ring like that."

Myrtle thought no more of it. Next day Tango was round Myrtle's house with the deposit. But the ring was a hundred pounds. Myrtle knew he'd never keep up the payments, but she couldn't find a way to say it to him, because he was very excited about getting Crystal the ring.

In a weak moment Myrtle accepted the money.

"I got really stuck," she says. "I was thinking I might send for the ring with Tango's deposit and then pay the rest of the instalments myself, so Mum wouldn't be let down taking bad debts, but I hadn't that sort of money."

"I suppose we could have had a whip round," Madonna says, but even she is doubtful about it. "Nobody had any money, and if we had, it would have been going to help Crystal and Baby D, not to buy a tacky sapphire ring from a catalogue so Tango could play the big man."

Myrtle held on to the money, while she was figuring out what to do, so Tango never got the special ring that Crystal so hankered after.

Probably that is where the petty cash money went, which would also explain why Tango was so evasive about it when Crystal got on to the subject. He'd taken the money to surprise her with the beautiful ring she was raving about, so he couldn't tell her, could he?

Getting the ring as a surprise for his dream woman is just the kind of stroke Tango would try to pull, but all it led to was a bewildered Crystal crying herself to sleep beside a sullen Tango.

They went to bed on it and they woke up on it. Baby D was crying and Crystal had to get out of bed to do his bottle. She was annoyed with Tango so she told him to get up and help her and he just humped up in the bed and wouldn't stir. Then she got blazing mad and chucked the saucepan at him. The boiling water went down the wall behind the bed.

Crystal couldn't take it any more.

She grabbed Baby D and went out into the hall but she couldn't go into the front room because that is where the Major sleeps at night. Mrs the Major slept in the third room across the hall because of her arthritis and his snoring. Crystal put Baby D in the pram Myrtle and Madonna had bought her second-hand in Tivi's shop and she banged out the door.

"I walked and walked and walked," she told Funny Bum. "I didn't know what to do."

Then she thought Baby D was getting cold and she would have to come back. She got as far as the corner of their street and when she did she saw a whole upset happening outside the Major's flat: two unmarked cars, one with the light going, and five cops round the front of the house.

"They took a bang at the basement door and they just rushed in," Crystal said. "So what I want to know is why were they doing that, breaking down the door and scaring everybody, when it was only Brian they were after?"

That's Crystal's version.

The Official Version is that they were hunting this man who had broken into a house and terrorized a poor crippled man on a sofa, threatening him with an iron bar.

How did the iron bar get into it? How can that be? Nobody knows.

"It was *me* spoke to Manus!" Funny Bum insists. "All I asked was was he all right, and later I told him I was sorry I'd disturbed him, something like that. I had nothing to hit him *with*. And he couldn't mistake me for Tango, could he? Tango's six foot; I'm five three on my good leg. And I'd no iron bar. Only my snakeskin bag, and that is nothing like an iron bar."

Whatever about that, the cops had their story. Manus was in hospital, sedated, because he'd hurt his back again rolling off the sofa so he could hide behind it, when he wasn't supposed to move or be moved except when he was lifted and laid.

"Maybe Manus regressed or something," Madonna says. "Like in one of those videos. He'd always been one to put the boot in, so he was used to thinking that way. Now he'd lost his strength, and he was scared stiff, thinking they'd come to cut him down. Although if he thought that, why did he tell everybody it was Tango? Why not the Bakulis?"

That's the charitable version, and it suggests an iron bar was used in the first attack when the Bakulis jumped him, although no one had heard of it before. We all understood Manus' back was hurt jumping off the landing to avoid the usual Bakuli beating. The alternative is to believe that someone at the O'Learys' decided to use the situation to have Tango put away. That's the malevolent version.

How it came to be said doesn't change what was said to the cops, hence the morning raid, as if Tango was a big drugs dealer or something.

"More cops than you'd ever see in one place," as Crystal related it afterwards.

They were running in and out of the basement and then Mrs the Major was out in her dressing-gown yelling at them and the poor old Major was sitting on the step wheezing.

"I was going down to help the Major," Crystal says.

Then Tango came out of the alley and grabbed her and before she knew what was happening Tango had her and the pram and he was heading off.

Bugging off in the face of the storm, as usual.

The cops hadn't got him, for the good reason that he'd put on his clothes and come out after Crystal because he reckoned she was jacking him in and going back to her mother's despite everything, and he wanted to stop her.

He was in his jeans and his pyjama top.

"Like somebody on the Big Breakfast!" Crystal told Funny Bum.

"That's it!" he told Crystal. "We're clearing off!"

And that's what they did.

CHAPTER SIXTEEN

Re-enter Sam-Sam, not too comfy at being visited by a detective with a little black hangman's book and a silver Parker pen his wife must have given him for Christmas.

"Young Brian Tangello is not my responsibility any more," Sam-Sam told him.

"What about the girl, Mr Samuelson?"

"Crystal is out of my jurisdiction as well," Sam-Sam said.

"Still of school age, according to her mother," the cop said.

"Well, you'd have to take that up with the Principal, Mrs. Evett," Sam-Sam said, stalling. "She's in the Austrian Tyrol, I believe. Back next week."

"Surely the school records…"

"Try the School Secretary," Sam-Sam told the cop, wishing him well of it, because Junky Allen never moves without Evett's say-so.

"We would welcome your co-operation, Mr Samuelson," the cop said, giving Sam-Sam a dirty look. "You taught both of them?"

"Yes."

"On drugs?"

"*No,*" firmly from Sam-Sam.

"Most of them are, Mr Samuelson."

"Not those two," Sam-Sam said.

"You're sure?"

"Well, nothing about them ever suggested it," Sam-Sam said. He felt pretty confident that was true. "Miss O'Leary ... Crystal ... she wasn't that type of girl."

"Just put it about a bit?"

"No, I don't believe so."

"Fifteen. And she's had a baby?" the cop said.

"I thought she was a decent kid," was all Sam-Sam said. "Not one of my troublemakers."

"But Tangello was?"

"Yes, Tangello was." There was no point denying it.

"Violent?"

"I wouldn't say that. He's big and he looks strong, but he was the sort who gets bullied, not the other way about," Sam-Sam said. "Look, he wasn't a star pupil, but I liked him. He was gentle."

The cop was getting impatient with him, because Sam-Sam wasn't saying what he was supposed to.

"This isn't just a domestic, Mr Samuelson,"

he said. "A sick man, almost a cripple, has been violently assaulted for the second time with a crowbar, in the safety of his own home."

"That doesn't sound like something Brian Tangello would do," was all Sam-Sam could say, thinking of Tango's long legs and his big stupid grin at the back of the class. "Tangello was ... is ... he's *soft*. And not very bright at the best of times. He'd, you know, nick a car for a run, that type of thing. But he would never take a crowbar to anyone."

"He did, Mr Samuelson ... twice."

"I don't believe that," flatly, from Sam-Sam.

"Look, Mr Samuelson: this started off as a family feud. We know Manus O'Leary is no angel. And we've filled in some of the details. We know O'Leary was after young Tangello for sleeping with his under-age sister, because Manus wrecked Tangello's aunt's house, hunting for him. Next thing we find is that Manus O'Leary has been badly beaten—"

"My understanding is that Tangello was the one who found him!" Sam-Sam interrupted.

"Yes. Tangello was there, or around. He even got a Miss Johnston to phone us for an ambulance – which is not like Miss Johnston. She's known to us as well. Tangello was covering his tracks. He also knew that he had O'Leary scared. *'Who did it, Manus?'* we asked him. O'Leary wouldn't speak. Then things get worse, and something happens, we don't know what, maybe something to do with Tangello's drug involvement, and Tangello loses the rag and decides to finish O'Leary off this time."

"Hold on," Sam-Sam said. "What drug involvement?"

"He's an associate of young Coney's, isn't he? That means either he's a dealer or a customer."

"He's neither," Sam-Sam said.

"Well, you're entitled to think what you like. We know what we know," the cop said.

"This is just fantasy, officer!" Sam-Sam said, getting belligerent. "I taught the boy. I know him. You're in a dream world."

"O'Leary was attacked, twice," the cop said. "Next time it could be murder. If you want to help Tangello, tell us where he is."

Sam-Sam shook his head.

The cop didn't like it.

"What makes me wonder is why you are so busy standing up for him when Tangello is a dangerous thug and a sneak thief, sleeping with one of your should-be pupils and going round trying to terrorize people with a crowbar. Next time it could be worse, Mr Samuelson. Miss O'Leary's baby could be at risk."

"Tangello would never hurt his baby," Sam-Sam said.

"His record of violence suggests that he well might!"

Sam-Sam could see he was making no headway. The cop had his version all written down in his little book of delusions, and Sam-Sam couldn't shake him.

"You'd better catch him and sort it out then, hadn't you?" he told the cop. "If big Tango is such a devil, you'd better clean him off the streets!"

So the cops got nothing out of Sam-Sam, or anybody else they tried. There was a fuss about it, with cops strutting round on a clean-up-the-Loop patrol, but nothing came of it.

Nobody – almost nobody – knew where Tango and Crystal and Baby D were.

Funny Bum must have known.

"Did Hank find them a place to hide, or was it some mate of Hank's hid them?" Madonna asked her once. Because despite the story about the petty cash, Hank still went on saying not-so-bad things about Tango.

"Don't know," Funny Bum stone-walled. "Why should I know?"

If it was Hank helping again then maybe that casts doubt on the story of Tango pinching the petty cash.

Funny Bum wasn't going to involve Hank, or anybody else. She had the same problem with the story of the intruder with the crowbar. The police had her down as part of the Tangello/Coney drugs gang that existed only in their own little notebook-minds, so they weren't going to take her word for what had happened against Manus' terror-stricken story. The only way she could prove her version was true was by involving the

Major, and she was too loyal to do that.

The next big development was Tango's grannie dying just when she did. That really mucked things up.

CHAPTER SEVENTEEN

Two months later, and Grannie T was laid out in her box.

Some old clergyman who had never seen her before was trying to talk about how she'd gone where the good grannies go.

On one side of the grave: Funny Bum, Mr and Mrs Hank's Autos, Madonna and Myrtle and Mrs Abjedi and a few hangers on who used to know Grannie T or Tango. On the other side, dolled up like a wax image of death herself, Auntie Flo Tangello, all on her own but for the woman who lived next door to her and the undertaker's man. I would have made the effort to be there for Tango's sake, but as it was (stuck up in Somerton), I didn't know Grannie T was dead. Come to that, I didn't even know Tango was a daddy, let alone that he'd bugged off with Crystal and the baby.

There had been a big bust up with the Welfare about who was to get the burial money. I don't know how it was sorted out. Funny Bum had no legal status, according to Louise Brennan, Tango wasn't to be found, and Auntie Flo refused to get involved in case she'd have to make a contribution. Meanwhile there was Mr Oki the undertaker with Grannie's corpse in his Shady Glade parlour, looking for grave money and money for the box out of somebody, only no one would pay up.

"If only the Major had been about, he'd have sorted it for me," Funny Bum said, but the Major had never been the same since the raid on his place. The police had turned the flat over looking for the drugs Tango was supposed to be trading in. Mrs the Major took it placidly enough, but the Major got worked up and indignant and ended up having a turn on the pavement outside the house. They had to get the bike medics out and oxygen to him. He was in a tent for a week and everybody thought he had snuffed it but he pulled round and they got him home. However, something had clicked over in his old head. He sat in his chair shivering and shaking and he was afraid to leave his flat. He wouldn't go out the door. He had new locks fitted front and back and big door bolts and Funny Bum had to do the shopping for them.

"You're very good to us, Miss Johnston," Mrs the Major said to her, and she never asked any questions about how Funny Bum came to be in such cahoots with the old man.

The only money forthcoming was from Myrtle, who handed the ring money Tango had given her over to Funny Bum. Myrtle had been really stuck with it, and was glad to have it off her conscience, considering she hadn't ordered the sapphire ring. She thought Tango wouldn't mind his Grannie T having the benefit of it.

The funeral money was sorted out with Sam-Sam's help and Grannie T was buried. Afterwards everybody was saying, "You'd have thought Tango would have been here, wouldn't you?"

So where was Tango, and why didn't he come?

"Stayed off, because he thought the cops would lift him," Jackie Coney said, and that was the general verdict in the San Marino, but it isn't what happened.

The true story, endorsed in outline by Funny Bum, is that Tango *did* come, and came what she calls "a long way". Tango had to scratch round to get the money for the train ticket and then when he'd got it he managed to get on a train that was re-routed because of some bomb scare on the line. He had to get off the train and hitched a lift in a lorry. It dropped him in the middle of nowhere. No one would pick him up because it was after dark. So he stayed the night in a bus shelter, catching a bus in the morning that took him into Caringby. From there he had to hoof it on foot.

Tango turned up at the cemetery gates just after his Grannie T was put in the ground. There was an unmarked car by the gate with some guy sitting in it, which he took for the cops, so he was afraid to go in.

He hid round the side till everyone had cleared off, and then he went into the cemetery alone.

He was up by the grave and a man came out of the office and started shouting at him, probably thinking he was going to nick Funny Bum's wreath the way people do.

"She's my grannie!" Tango tried telling the man.

"And I'm Greta Garbo's ghost!" the man told him.

Then Tango ran off because the man was talking about calling the cops, and the last thing Tango wanted was the cops.

Where did Tango go then? The most likely place is Funny Bum's flat, but if he did go there she wasn't in because she was at the Major's place helping Mrs the Major sort things out, and after that she was in the Builders' Arms, and she didn't get back till past seven.

The funeral was over at half past three; that is when they all left the cemetery.

The next sighting of Tango by anyone who knew him is nearly eleven o'clock at night, so what did he do? It was raining most of the afternoon, and he was afraid to go up round the Loop so maybe he went to the pictures, if he had the money. He might have gone down by the canal, where it is quiet, and just hung around by their love seat, looking at the water – though seven hours is lot of hanging around. What was he *doing* all that time? Probably he hid out in the Milkwhite Bread container, his old bedroom with the ripped metal side and the rusty doors, huddling down amid the beer cans and hugging his big knees to keep warm.

Night-time, 132 Bright Street, Auntie Flo's house:

"I opened the door wearing my dressing-gown, and there he was, pale as a sheet, and weepy," Auntie Flo told me.

"You?" she said to him. "Brian?"

"Yeah."

"What do you want?"

"I want in," Tango said.

"Well, I don't want you in."

He shoved past her, through the doorway and into the hall.

"I am in," he started to say, and the next thing she knew he began to sob and cry and Auntie Florence, give her her due, shut the door and shovelled him into her front room, putting him down in an armchair by the fire, which she'd just banked up before going to bed.

Then she made him a cup of tea.

"I just wanted to see you again," Tango said.

"Yes, Brian," she said.

"Were you ... did you...?"

"I was," she said.

"Only there's only you and me left, knew her proper," Tango said, which sounds odd given that Funny Bum had been looking after the old lady month after month after month, lifting her and laying her and doing the doings with the portaloo.

"That's right, Brian," Auntie Flo said.

"What'll I do?" Tango said. "Why did this happen?"

"Well, people do die, Brian," Auntie Flo said. "It can't be helped. And she was a good age. She'd had her time."

"I didn't want her to die. I never wanted her to die!"

"You were very good to her, Brian," Auntie Flo said.

"I wasn't. I never…" and he started to cry again.

"Oh come on, big Brian," Auntie Flo said, and she went and sat down beside him and put her arm around him.

"I don't want you!" he said, shaking it off. "It's her I want. My gran."

There wasn't a lot she could say to that.

"I love my grannie. I love my gran!"

This went on for a bit … well, more than a bit. He was rambling on, almost incoherently at times, about his old gran this and his old grannie that and how he had let her down and not looked after her properly and how he should have come down only he didn't know she was going to die until she was dead and then he was late because Crystal was told and Crystal didn't tell him until the night before.

"Why ever not?" Auntie Flo said. "Why did she keep it from you?"

"I didn't see her Monday," he said. "I'm supposed to see her Monday when the woman's

160

there but I didn't go because I had a bit of bother. I tried to phone her but the woman didn't give her the message and Crystal got out without them knowing and she went looking for me but she didn't know about the bother I was in and she went to the wrong place and she couldn't find me."

"Hold on, Brian," Auntie Flo said. "Out of where? Where are Crystal and the wee baby?"

"They're all right," was all he would say at first. Then he added proudly, "I've seen to it that my baby's looked after proper now!"

And he showed her a photo he had in his wallet – which, by her account, had about thirty pounds in it. She took that in, Auntie Flo being Auntie Flo. She was relieved by it, because she had suspected he'd come for money.

The photo was of Crystal and Baby D.

"I go to see them every day the woman will let me," he said, proudly.

"Is the O'Leary girl ... Crystal ... is she in some kind of hostel?" Auntie Flo asked. "Is that where your baby's being looked after? In some kind of off-the-street place?"

But he clammed up.

"You never liked Crystal," he said.

"True enough, Brian," Auntie Flo admitted. "I've little time for either of you. But the child's a different matter. Does the old woman O'Leary know what has happened to her grandson? Is she not ashamed enough to want to do something about it?"

161

"D's *my* baby," Tango said. "My baby. Do you think I don't know that?"

"Well that's fine, if you can manage to look after him," Auntie Flo said.

"I'm not looking for help from anyone," he said, with just a touch of the old swagger in his voice, though it came and went all in the one sentence.

"Good," she said. "Because you'll not get any in this house, anyway!"

She thought he was going to start yelling and cursing at her, the way he sometimes did when he was at home, but he just subsided back onto the sofa. He had his glasses off, because he'd been mopping his eyes with his shirt sleeve, and the glasses were on the floor. He got them up on his nose and lay back, gazing up at the print of a Cherokee Indian on her wall, which she is very proud of. Since she'd had Tango and Grannie T out of her house she'd been able to do it up properly, for the first time ever, she says, because they were costing her money instead of giving her money, and taking up a lot of room.

"I'd like to stay here tonight, Auntie Flo," he said.

She took a deep breath.

"I don't want you here, Brian."

"Oh."

"I let you in because I was sorry for you," she said, which wasn't strictly true of course – he had barged his way in. "But I don't want you staying here in my house."

162

"*Your* house?" he said. "It's supposed to be my home."

"No, Brian," she said. "Not any longer."

Deep silence.

"You want rid of me then?"

"Yes. I think you should go."

His eyes welled up.

"You'll not tell anyone I've been here?" he said. "I don't want them after me and Crystal any more, now we're maybe beginning to get things together again."

"I won't tell anyone," she said, though she wasn't sure what she was supposed to be not telling.

"Baby D must have the two that loves him, not anyone else," he said, "and Crystal knows that. So we're going to make it work for the sake of my baby, I told her. And it will work, if they all keep out of it."

"Right, Brian."

"Don't you go telling old Mrs O there's been trouble," he said. "I don't want her sticking her nose in it, after my baby. Not again."

"I'm not going to tell anybody anything, Brian," she said. "But I want you to go, please."

So he went off into the night, but not before Auntie Flo *says* she relented and gave him a cheque for seventy-five pounds, representing his cut of the money she had got for selling some of Grannie T's old things.

"If you believe that, you'll believe anything!"

163

Jackie Coney says. "What good is a cheque to somebody like Tango?"

Whatever about that, whether it is true or not, my guess would be that Auntie Flo didn't keep her word to Tango.

She found her way round to Stanley Street a few nights later and confronted Mrs O and Sister Monica Rose with her half-news about Mrs O's daughter and grandson. Did she find out more from Tango than she is telling? Did she put Sister Monica Rose and her Geek on the trail of Crystal and the baby?

"Well, it would figure!" Madonna says. "But that isn't the way Crystal told it at the time, and I don't think she had any reason to lie, though her story did change a bit later. By Crystal's account she came home of her own accord because she couldn't take living with Tango and his tricks any more. He'd hurt her and hurt her – not always meaning to, but doing it just the same, though he was maybe too muddled up to know how he was doing it – and she'd been lied to and deceived and let down once too often by his big talk that never got anywhere."

That's supposed to be why Crystal came home alone, bringing Tango's precious baby with her.

If Crystal mentioned her *Tony* at all, Madonna didn't pick up on it at that stage. Tony was Crystal's little secret. Once he came on the scene Crystal had a whole new agenda, and Tango wasn't part of it, but she wasn't going to highlight

164

that, talking to Madonna. When Tony's name did come up, subsequently, Crystal underplayed it for Madonna's benefit. She never wanted that bit of her story stressed round the Loop, because the Crystal it shows up is very different from the ex-Goody Club Crystal she wanted Madonna to see, and believe in.

CHAPTER EIGHTEEN

The Crystal who arrived back at Mrs O's wasn't like the old Crystal.

"She was smoking a lot," Madonna says. "I know she smoked before, Chris, but this was different. Puff-puff-puff-puff. She had me gassed." How did that happen? Tango never smoked, so she can't have got it from him.

"The smoking started after she met Tango," Madonna says. "You can make what you like of that. Trying to be more grown up for his benefit, perhaps."

That's odd with Tango's known feelings about things like smoking which had made him stand out from Jackie and Stevie and the mob. That last year at William Whitlaw most people were at it, and many had been at it from Form One. William Whitlaw was that way, despite all Evett's posters in the corridors and Sam-Sam's talks. Evett made him do the talks because someone had to do them, and she knew we knew Sam-Sam smoked his pipe when he was off the premises. Evett only did it to make Sam-Sam squirm.

"After a bit, she let slip about this guy Tony." Madonna's voice dipped when she talked about him. "Crystal didn't mean to mention him, but it slipped out of her. Tony had been good to her and the baby when Brian sloped off, that kind of thing. So I said to her, "Tango sloped off?" because it didn't sound right. "Tango dumped you and Baby D?"

Crystal went all funny, Madonna says.

"When I went in that place," she said.

"What place?"

"Just a place. Where me and my baby could get looked after. Because we had no money, and we hadn't no proper place, and Brian said Baby D had to have somewhere. 'I don't want to go in no place like that,' I told him, but Brian said the baby was most important of all. So I had to go in so they could look after D because of his little chest, like."

Madonna hadn't heard that the baby had respiratory problems before, and she said so. I think it is interesting that Crystal's version, amended from the truth for Madonna's benefit, has Tango giving her orders again. At that stage the idea of Tango giving Crystal orders and Crystal meekly doing what she was told is just a laugh, as far as I am concerned.

"The cold got at him, my poor little D," Crystal said, holding him on her knee. "The place we was in was damp and leaky, just the one room with this crumbly old yellow paper peeling off the wall. There was twenty people all piled in on the one stair, and just the one stinky toilet and no bath and a little gas cooker on the landing, so you smelt other people's dinners all the time and it was ... it wasn't nice. So Brian made me go to this other place, where D would be safe when he had this little wheezy thing in his throat, and his rash. But he's all right now. Aren't you, D?"

Note the "Brian made me" touch again.

Baby D smiled at her, (though it may have been wind).

"You're my lovely wee baby," she told him.

"So who was Tony?" Madonna asked.

"Well, he kind of fancied me," Crystal said, as if it was a joke, but she was odd about it.

"Tony and Brian had a go at each other," she said. "Brian got his glasses smashed and Tony turned vicious. So I told Tony, 'clear off and leave me alone' and he cleared off, Tony did. Brian thought I was still seeing Tony when I wasn't. Only the way we were, it was difficult, because Tony was about all the time, wasn't he? His wife was in the same place I was in, but they didn't get on, so Tony tried it on with the others, it wasn't just me."

This is the nearest Crystal got to telling the truth to Madonna. She may have *needed* to say it to someone to get it off her chest, but perhaps I am giving her too much credit. It adds up to a cover story that still has Madonna fooled, despite all I've told her.

Crystal stopped and tickled the baby a bit, then she started off again. Madonna admits the vibes coming off Crystal weren't good.

"They wouldn't let my Brian come round like Tony in the day because he hadn't his P...? Whatever that form is. He didn't show up anywhere on their sodding computer, did he? That meant we had to make out I was on my own with the baby and he'd dumped me, even though he didn't dump me, but for me to get in the place we had to make out he did, and he really didn't like it, Brian didn't."

That seemed to be important to her.

"He really loves me, Brian does." Crystal was still insisting.

"Well, then, you should be with him!" Madonna said.

"No. I can't. No way," from Crystal.

"Why not? If Tango ... if *Brian* loves you and you love him?"

"It wasn't just Tony," Crystal said awkwardly. "It was me. When you have your baby you think it will make no difference. But it does."

"Well, I don't see that," Madonna said, thinking Crystal had gone off at a tangent.

"You might if it happened to you," Crystal said. "Brian wants to be a daddy all right. He ... he wants it so much in his head, but when it comes to doing it, he cops out. Like I mean he's always going to do this or that or get this or that for the baby but it doesn't happen, does it? Except it happens in his head as if he thinks he has done it, or maybe he will do it tomorrow, but tomorrow turns out to be just the same. Brian really loves my baby, but he mucks everything up. If you find you can't rely on somebody and it happens again and again and again, each time it happens and things are getting worse you begin to think, 'Why am I staying with this person? This person is hopeless.' And then you find you don't love them the way you thought you did ... like all the time love them, so you can be with them."

Then she must have thought she'd said enough to colour things the way she wanted them to seem to Madonna, and she stopped talking about it.

"She'd gone off Tango and she'd gone on this Tony for a bit, and this Tony had dumped her," is what Madonna makes of that, but I believe it went a lot further than Crystal was letting on.

Whatever the cause, it hadn't done Crystal much good. Trailing up and down Stanley Street with the baby in the push-chair, she wasn't an elf-like little figure any more. She had filled out, in the face mostly, and her hair was dyed a kind of coral colour. She wore grotty clothes and scuffed white pumps with low heels.

"I felt really sorry for her," Madonna says. "She was trapped in that house with Manus and her mother and all of them taking their orders from Sister Monica Rose and her Geek."

Sister Monica Rose and the Geek had moved in

170

when Crystal left, though they didn't operate the full service from the house in Stanley Street, as they had from the flat. This possibly supports Jackie Coney's story about them being chucked out of the flat in Shaftesbury. When Crystal came back, they didn't move out. They were very good, Sister and the Geek, Crystal says. They'd taken over looking after both Manus and Crystal's mother, but life in Number 8 was a kind of constant prayer meeting. The Geek sat in Manus' room and Sister Monica Rose was in and out washing his feet.

"My mum's a kind of sideshow in her own home," Crystal said. "Those two got her right where they want her, haven't they? She reckons they've made Manus all right, and anybody can see that poor Manus is never going to be all right, and she falls for it. He doesn't even talk any more, Manus. Just lies there while they say their prayers and when they go out he gets me to put on the TV and he watches that all bloody day till Sister comes in, and then she puts it off and and she's praying at him again, and it makes me want to throw up."

"Well, I think that is terrible!" Madonna told her.

"Oh, no," Crystal said. "Sister and the Geek are good people. They may be mad, but they aren't con artists. They believe in what they are doing. It isn't terrible at all."

"Why isn't it terrible? They're pulling the wool over your mother's eyes, and they've taken over your house."

"Because it's made Mum feel right," Crystal said. "Mum is back being happy inside. Well not back, really, this is different. Happy inside like she never was before, even with Manus in the house like a spare baby. So I don't want to go sounding off about Sister and the Geek, do I? They pay their way. And I'm in no position to complain after what I put Mum through. I am stuck with it. Till I can work something out, I am."

"What sort of something?"

"Dunno," Crystal said, and the way she said it Madonna didn't think that Crystal was even looking to see what it might be.

"She'd given in, that's all," Madonna says. "I don't know what she had been through with Tango and this Tony, but it had knocked the stuffing out of Crystal, and all the hope at the same time."

That was the scenario Tango came back into.

"He just landed on my doormat," Funny Bum says. "Friday evening he came banging the door, no notice, out of the night. He was all weird, not talking much, lugging a big bag."

"You come back to square things with Crystal?" Funny Bum asked him, because she thought he had.

"She don't want me," Tango said. "She has this fella."

"No, she hasn't," Funny Bum said. Madonna had filled her in on the Tony story and how Crystal had said it was all over and done with – which, of

172

course, it was by then, but that didn't help Tango much.

"Crystal loves you, Tango," Funny Bum told him, despite the evidence. "But you've got to straighten all this stuff out, haven't you?"

"I haven't done nothing," Tango said.

"Well, a lot of people think you have," Funny Bum said.

"I never."

"You straighten yourself out first, then you have a go at Crystal," Funny Bum suggested.

"How?" Tango said, bleakly.

"I don't know what you've been at, what annoyed her. So how can I say how?" Funny Bum said. "You shake yourself up, Tango, because she needs you."

"I'm not here for that," Tango told her.

He was telling her that he had at long last accepted that Crystal didn't love him and never would love him again – which marked a big break in Tango's mind, given the obsessive way he had kept after her from their first days at school. Funny Bum the romantic didn't want to hear that message, so she didn't hear it. She wanted it to be like the soaps on TV.

"Well, what are you here for?" Funny Bum said.

"I'm just here," he said, head down, not looking at her at all.

Then he said, "My baby."

"What about the baby?"

"D is *my* baby," he said.

"Yeah. He is your baby," Funny Bum said.

"Well, some people don't say so any more," he said.

"I think he was talking about Crystal," Madonna says. "Crystal wanted Baby D all to herself, because she couldn't cope with Tango. Crystal had taken his baby from him. D is mine, not yours, is what she was saying, as if D was a virgin birth. Tango knew he was the natural father, Crystal never disputed that, but she wouldn't accept that he had any claim on her child."

Long silence.

"I know I lost Crystal, see?" Tango told Funny Bum "I lost Crystal but I want my baby!"

Then he clammed up on her. You'd think that the way he was talking would have been warning enough for most people, but Funny Bum didn't fix on it. She thought he was upset, maybe a bit off his trolley, but in the morning they would talk it over and perhaps she could sort him out, and stop him doing anything silly.

It would all come right in the end, just like in the soaps. Nobody would get hurt, completely contrary to her own experience of life, but then she hadn't accepted her own experience either. It was all going to come right tomorrow: she would get her kids back, Tango and Crystal and Baby D would live happily ever after, and the sun would shine on Buffey's Loop for ever more, Amen.

"Tango slept the Friday night on my sofa, and Saturday afternoon he went and done it." Funny

174

Bum says. "If I'd known what he was going to do I would have stopped him, even if I had to break my good leg to do it."

It is doubtful if she could have stopped Tango anyway.

CHAPTER NINETEEN

Crystal had the baby out shopping in the little blue suit Sister bought him, and they went into Tesco's.

Sister Monica Rose's old baldy Geek was along, looking for artichokes, and handing people his little tracts. He always did that. He would stand round and shove his hand-outs at people, like he was running a Charity Prize Draw or something, only there wasn't a prize, just his self-authorized version of the Good News according to the Geek. It embarrassed Crystal the first few times she was out with him, because they'd walk back the way they had come and there would be his Good News in the gutter, but she says she'd got used to it.

Tango must have followed the trail of tracts down the High Street, without Crystal or the Geek seeing him, waiting his chance.

Crystal got her things, the Geek hand-picked his artichokes, and they were lined up at the checkout.

D was strapped into the baby seat of the trolley.

They got to the front of the queue. Crystal put her things on the belt. The Geek was behind her counting the ten ps in his little purple purse with the zip top. He was shop-side of the checkout, waiting till the girl had flicked Crystal's stuff over her electronic eye.

Crystal pushed the empty trolley through, with Baby D on it.

"I was watching Lily on the till," she told Madonna. "Brian must have been hiding near the door. There were these cartons piled up. Maybe he was behind them. Or maybe he stood in the door of the office, like he was waiting for the manager, only I didn't see him."

She was watching the bill mount up when someone ran past her, banging into her so she went off balance, and the someone grabbed hold of her trolley with the baby on it.

"Brian!" she screamed.

And she was after him.

Tango reached the exit and spun the trolley through the door. Crystal grabbed the end of the trolley furthest from the baby and she yanked it, pulling it back towards her.

Tango had his hand on the baby, and the trolley went towards Crystal and away from him, so that D was caught by the clip and strap, halfway out of the little seat.

"I thought, 'My baby'll pull apart!'" Crystal told Madonna.

"Brian!" she screamed again.

He was fumbling, but he must have undone the clip, because he got the baby free.

He didn't say anything.

He shoved the trolley at her.

She was still holding it, so when he shoved it he was shoving her, and she stumbled.

"He was too quick for me!" Crystal says.

Tango was out of the door and away, with Baby D in his arms.

"Brian! Brian! My baby!" Crystal yelled, and the Geek woke up and threw his artichokes at Lily and pushed his way past the till, heading for the door. By the time they were both outside Tesco's all they could see were people milling up and down the High Street.

"Brian had vanished into thin air," Crystal says. "And he had my baby. D was gone and I'm running and yelling and shrieking and people are looking at me and getting in the way and Brian is so big but I couldn't even see him so I don't know what he did or how he did it, whether he went in some shop or what, because all I could see was people and people and people and none of them was Brian and none of them was my baby and I'm pushing and shoving and trying to see."

And that was it.

The baby was gone.

The security man from Tesco's who should have been on the door stopping shoplifters or baby snatchers was out trying to calm Crystal down and

Crystal was standing in the road screaming and screaming and screaming, wanting to run, but not knowing which way to go.

A crowd gathered, treating Crystal as a side-show in a funfair or street entertainment, which in a way she was. They were all having a bit of drama with their weekend shopping, but nobody was helping her.

"I can't imagine anything worse than that happening," Madonna says. "Doing that to her is the one thing I never, never will forgive old Tango for. I don't care if he was a screw loose when he did it, there is no excuse for that."

"This young woman's had her baby stolen," the Geek told the Tesco manager when he came out.

They got on the phone and the cops came and there were people saying they saw someone carrying a baby. People seemed to be seeing babies everywhere.

"The cops were brilliant!" Jackie Coney says, and if Jackie says that then they were, because Jackie isn't a cop fan.

Cops everywhere, through the whole place like a dose of salts, Beltown and the Loop.

Funny Bum came home to find them hunting through her flat. The Major's was raided too, and half a dozen other houses round the Loop. They were up to the school, and round the waste ground, and swarming down by the canal where Tango used to go when he was upset. They were round the bus station and the railway looking and stopping and

179

searching and manhandling every baby in sight.

So how about Hank's?

There *were* cops through Hank's within an hour of the baby going missing, they were that quick, but Hank says that they didn't seem to know what they were doing. He swears he told them about the Milkwhite Bread container and they went down the yard to search it, but then they got a message through that the baby was found and all right. That stopped them. They went away. Later it turned out to be some other baby.

The Milkwhite Bread container is where Baby D and Tango were.

"I thought the cops might have missed something," Hank says. "So I went and checked round the yard myself, later."

He was poking about with his torch, and he wandered down towards the canal end, where the container was.

There was a faint light showing under the doors of the container.

"Jesus!" Hank thought.

He went back to his office and phoned the cops. He told them there was a light coming out of the container and it was the one that Tango used to use.

"So you'd better come back here quickly, because I think Tango might be in it with the baby!" Hank told the cops. No messing about *not* calling the cops, you'll note. It's different when you come to a thing like that, with a baby.

So the cops came.

The first thing one of them said to Hank was, "Is any of your stuff missing?"

"What stuff?" said Hank.

"Fuel," the cop said. "Old junk, particularly any inflammable materials. Stuff like that. You get my drift?"

Hank got it in one.

His yard is falling down with things like that, because of stripping down the innards of the old autos, and there is plenty of petrol about the place. If somebody wanted to start a blaze, Hank's would be the place to do it.

"Tango wouldn't," he said. "He'd never hurt the baby."

"They sometimes do," the cop said. "And it wouldn't be a new idea round here, would it?"

"He wouldn't!" Hank insisted.

"If the boy is going round stealing babies…" the cop said, and he left Hank to think about it.

The place filled up with cops and cars. There was an ambulance and a doctor, a little man who sat in Hank's office all wrapped in a big coat.

"Tango loves that baby," Hank told him.

"That could be just the problem," the doctor said.

The cops had Livingstone Road cordoned off at both ends.

Jackie Coney has it that there were cops with guns too, down the canal bank, working their way to the far side of the container, and I suppose that that would have to be right. Jackie was sure Tango would be shot, like on TV.

When you think about it from the cops' point of view, it was a real puzzler. A boy and baby inside a rusty container in the dark. They have it in their heads that the boy has a record of violence, that he's broken up with his family and his girlfriend, that he has stolen her baby, and that he is kinked and unstable at the best of times, a genuine product of Buffey's Loop.

If we make a mistake, they'd be thinking, *he'll kill himself and the baby.*

Hence the guns and the lights and the cars and the ambulance and the doctor and the special medics on their motorbikes.

"Don't kill my baby!" Crystal's moment of fame on the news.

Hank says they tried shouting at the container, from a safe distance, using loudhailers. No response.

"Would you mind if we used your office, Hank?" a big cop said, and they bundled Hank out of it, behind the lines.

Some conference with a bigwig cop.

More loudhailers.

"I wanted to go down. I wanted them to let me talk to Brian, but they wouldn't," Crystal says. One of the cops told Sister Monica Rose that they thought Crystal might go hysterical and set Tango off, and then she might go up in flames with Tango and the baby, because Tango would want to kill her too. That was the way the cops saw it.

"We're way up the road by the barrier," Madonna says. "And we're waiting for somebody to shoot Tango, or for the container to go up in flames if Tango used a lighter, the way everybody thought he was planning to."

The next thing anybody knew the cops were opening the big gates down the side of Dock Road that Hank usually keeps closed.

Out came a police van.

The policeman on the barrier got the crowds to stand back and the van slowed till he had done it. Then he waved it through, and it was away down the road to the cop shop.

Tango was in it, but nobody knew that.

Other cop vehicles were coming out of Hank's – minibuses, and cars. Then the ambulance pulled out, only not in a hurry. It looked like nobody was in it, but Tango's baby was.

Tango went one way.

Baby D went the other.

So what had happened?

They showed the inside of the container on TV, and it was really weird.

There were baby posters and a blue fluffy mat with a pink lion design laid on the floor, and a cushion, and D's old blue teddy bear that Tango and Crystal had for the first Christmas, and some baby food in a tin that didn't look as if it had been touched, and the duvet Tango had wrapped himself and the baby in, and a candle stuck in the

183

neck of a bottle, so he could see his baby's face smiling at him.

Then this cop came on. He was the one credited with rescuing the baby.

"He was sitting there holding the baby," the cop said. "I said, 'Brian?' He just looked at me. I said, 'Brian, will you give me the baby now?' He said, 'It's my baby.' I said, 'Yes, Brian. But Crystal needs to feed the baby.' He said, 'Yes.' 'You'll give me the baby, Brian?' I said. 'Yes,' he said. Then he got up and he came over to the door and he handed me the baby out and I said: 'That's a good boy, Brian.'"

That's a good boy, Brian.

"Just like Tango was a baby himself," Madonna says. "I bet that poor cop was sweating!"

CHAPTER TWENTY

The TV and the tabloids had their day, at Tango's expense. Most of the stuff they printed was rubbish; the Loop came out as a sink estate, and we were all joyriding junkies living off the Welfare.

Crystal got all the sympathy; teenage single mum bravely coping, that line. They trapped her into saying all kinds of stuff, but then she wasn't built to cope with that pressure. I don't blame her for it, but the whole thing was tilted her way, against Tango – the big guy got slagged, and I knew that couldn't be right.

The sun was beating down and the Loop was looking good. I had cornered Crystal and the baby, because I wasn't going to let her keep avoiding me, however much she wanted to.

She was down on the love-seat by the canal where they had their first tryst. She must have sneaked out for a quick puff. Sister Monica Rose wouldn't let her smoke in the house.

"Look, I've had enough of you, Chris, right?" she said. "What's wrong with you? Why do you bloody keep pestering me? I've got nothing more I'm going to say to you. I never did like you and I'm fed up with you going round asking questions, trying to make out I am to blame for everything. Tango's had his day in court, and now he's lounging about on a season ticket in a nice comfy prison, right? But I'm the one that's left out here doing time! What is it with you anyway? Why can't you just let it go?"

"I'll tell you why," I said. "You did for poor Tango, that's why. Now you're doing goody-two-shoes and his name is muck, all over the papers, and I don't see why you should get away with it."

"Look, I'm not staying here to listen to this stuff!" she said, angrily. "Everybody's told you – you're making this stuff up on me. Me and Tony and all. And it's not bloody fair and I've had enough of you." Her voice trailed away.

"Sod you, Chris, for a rotten little sod!" she muttered, collecting the baby in her arms.

"OK," I said. "Tell me about Tony, then."

"Sod Tony!" she said. "What do you want me to tell you? How he got in my knickers, is that it, so you can have a thrill?" She dropped her fag by her feet, and ground it out with the heel of her shoe. "So what? What if he did? I fancied him and I didn't fancy Brian no more. 'Cause he could do things Brian couldn't. Is that what you want me to say?"

"I thought it was something like that," I said.

"Yeah, well, didn't happen, did it? It wasn't like that. He was no good to me neither, just like Brian. Because I can't pick them, can I? I get Brian who can't handle stuff and I think he's great, then I get Tony and I think I'm landed, but it turns out he's just flash, Tony. One week out of that place, and he dumps me. Like he's got what he wanted. Gone! So it serves me right. That makes me to blame for everything, I suppose."

"You dumped Tango and went off with this Tony and you took the big guy's baby with you!" I said.

"Of course I took the bloody baby!" she said. "What do you think I am? Little D is my baby! I'm the one that looks after me and him. Brian never could, for all his talk."

"You took Tango's baby off him," I repeated. "He was no use to you, was he? But it was Brian-Big-Deal when your daddy died and Tango was the one picked you off the floor; it was 'My Brian' this and 'My Brian' that and he was your dream come true and you were going to love him for ever. Then you decide that he's not going to make it and you dump him, cold. He's told to bog off, just the same as when we were at school in the playcage."

She stood there, clinging to her baby. Little D's fat face gurgled up at me.

"You've been making up all this dirty stuff about me, Chris," she said. "Going round asking questions off my friends, slagging me."

187

"Tango was my mate," I told her.

"Yeah, well..." she said. "You didn't help him much then, did you?"

"I wasn't here. My dad moved us, remember? I never knew what was going on. I just know you were the big number in his life. Right from the start, at school. Everybody knows that. He got you, and there was the baby, and he had it made. He's up there riding a rainbow ... and you took it all away from him."

"It's none of your bloody business!" Crystal said angrily. "Sod you, sod school, sod everybody."

"Sod Tango too?" I said, because I wasn't letting her off with it that easy. "You really knotted the poor guy up, didn't you? But you're OK. You're getting on with your life. You got what you needed off him. Now he's flushed down the pan and you—"

"Me? I'm left holding the baby," she said, sourly.

"*His* baby," I said. "Tango's."

Crystal's face flushed, and she took a firmer grip on Baby D, balancing him against the angle of her hip.

"You go on about trying to understand what's happened," she said, slowly, "but you've just made up what it might have been like between me and Brian. Don't you never go falling in love with someone, Chris, 'cause you'll find it works out a lot more complicated than you think. Dangerous old game, love is, when you can't handle it."

"Yeah," I said. "*For Tango,* it was."

There was a long pause. Her eyes were shiny, and her pale cheeks were moist, suddenly.

"You're *crying,* Crystal?" I said.

"Yeah," she said. "Are you satisfied now, Chris?"

"Crystal's right. You can't find out what really happened, Chris," Madonna said when we talked about it. "You don't live in her skin or his, so there's no point in trying to score points against the poor little thing. Leave her alone. You'll never understand what went on between those two. No outsider ever does. Maybe they don't understand it themselves."

"I know Tango was the one who got hammered," I said.

"He was always going to," Madonna said.

THE KIDNAPPING OF SUZIE Q
Martin Waddell

At 4.35 Suzie Quinn is a shopper in her local supermarket. At 4.43 she's a kidnap victim.

One afternoon Suzie Quinn and her mum dash into their local supermarket, planning to be in and out as quickly as possible. Minutes later, while Suzie waits at the checkout, two robbers hold up the store. They too have planned a speedy getaway. But no one has planned for what happens next: after a brief struggle, Suzie finds herself taken hostage by the desperate gang. Now she is Suzie Q, headline kidnap victim, and must summon every ounce of courage and cunning to survive.

This is a dramatic and nail-biting thriller by double Smarties Book Prize Winner, Martin Waddell.

MORE WALKER PAPERBACKS
For You to Enjoy

☐ 0-7445-7862-0   *Starry Night*
                    by Martin Waddell   £3.99

☐ 0-7445-7824-8   *The Beat of the Drum*
                    by Martin Waddell   £3.99

☐ 0-7445-8211-3   *Frankie's Story*
                    by Martin Waddell   £3.99

☐ 0-7445-6989-3   *The Kidnapping of Suzie Q*
                    by Martin Waddell   £3.99

☐ 0-7445-7791-8   *Burger Wuss*
                    by M.T. Anderson   £3.99

☐ 0-7445-5484-5   *Fire, Bed and Bone*
                    by Henrietta Branford   £3.99

☐ 0-7445-4191-3   *Monkey*
                    by Veronica Bennett   £3.99

☐ 0-7445-7240-1   *The Burning Baby
                    and Other Ghosts*
                    by John Gordon   £3.99

**Walker Paperbacks are available from most booksellers,
or by post from B.B.C.S., P.O. Box 941, Hull, North Humberside HU1 3YQ**

24 hour telephone credit card line 01482 224626

To order, send: Title, author, ISBN number and price for each book ordered, your full
name and address, cheque or postal order payable to BBCS for the total amount and
allow the following for postage and packing: UK and BFPO: £1.00 for the first book,
and 50p for each additional book to a maximum of £3.50. Overseas and Eire: £2.00 for
the first book, £1.00 for the second and 50p for each additional book.

Prices and availability are subject to change without notice.

Name _____

Address _____

_____